Joan -
You were the beginning — Now read the rest of the story —

Your friend,
Rhonda

Book #1

Catch a Falling Star

RHONDA BURNAUGH

Order this book online at www.trafford.com
or email orders@trafford.com

Most Trafford titles are also available at major online book retailers.

© Copyright 2014 Rhonda Burnaugh.

All rights reserved. No part of this publication may be reproduced, stored in a retrieval system, or transmitted, in any form or by any means, electronic, mechanical, photocopying, recording, or otherwise, without the written prior permission of the author.

Printed in the United States of America.

ISBN: 978-1-4907-3509-2 (sc)
ISBN: 978-1-4907-3511-5 (hc)
ISBN: 978-1-4907-3510-8 (e)

Library of Congress Control Number: 2014907991

Because of the dynamic nature of the Internet, any web addresses or links contained in this book may have changed since publication and may no longer be valid. The views expressed in this work are solely those of the author and do not necessarily reflect the views of the publisher, and the publisher hereby disclaims any responsibility for them.

Any people depicted in stock imagery provided by Thinkstock are models, and such images are being used for illustrative purposes only.
Certain stock imagery © Thinkstock.

Trafford rev. 05/08/2014

Trafford PUBLISHING® www.trafford.com

North America & international
toll-free: 1 888 232 4444 (USA & Canada)
fax: 812 355 4082

*Dedicated to
Doug, the first person to endure my obsession,
April, the first official reader, advisor, and editor in chief,
Christian, who offered great ideas and great patience with me,
Samantha, my cheerleader,
and Nancy, my best friend and the person who told
me to go for it, because if it weren't for her,
I wouldn't have pursued my dream of writing.
Thanks to all of you for your support and encouragement.*

After class, she followed him down the hallway to his locker. "Hey. Do you like what you see?"

"Hey, you." He smiled back at her. "Maybe."

"I'm Seraphine."

He closed his locker door and turned to face her. "Lovely name. What does it mean?"

"It's Hebrew. It designates a special class of heavenly attendants in God's court."

"I'm Michael, who is like God."

"You're either very confident or extremely egotistical." Sera stood tall.

He laughed. "I meant in Hebrew that is what my name means. I wasn't trying to make a statement. By the way, if you're a heavenly attendant, doesn't that mean you're an angel?"

She blushed. "There's only one way to know. You'd have to get to know me."

Michael leaned against his locker. "So are you doing anything after school today?"

* * *

Michael thought it was cool she was Native American and loved listening to her talk about her culture. They often walked home together, as they lived only a few blocks apart. He enjoyed playing his guitar for her, and she liked making him lunch, because a lot of the time, he showed up at school with nothing to eat and that made her sad.

Sera spent more and more of her time at Michael's home. Her mother didn't seem to care, and Michael's mother was, by any diagnostic tool, two hundred pounds of flat-out crazy. When Michael's mother refused to take her medication, which was most of the time, she was in and out of psychiatric facilities.

Michael had warned Sera, when his mother started loudly singing religious hymns and talking to people who weren't there, it was time to hurdle out of the window, or as he put it: *She's gonna blow.* Gina was in charge, which was to say, Michael wasn't even

Prologue

1996

Marysville, California: Population: 12,072, give or take a few. Home of the Marysville Vikings. Mascot: Indians. Colors: orange and black. Halloween lasts year-round. Fifty-six percent of the high school students are white. Four percent are black. Twenty-three percent are Hispanic. The rest don't care or don't know who they are. California produces about 70 percent of the world's prunes. With almost one-third of California's plum acreage in Yuba and Sutter counties, the area rightfully claims the proud title of Prune Capital of the World. The festival also features the annual Prune Run . . .

* * *

What seemed like a lifetime ago, Seraphine and Michael were best friends. Michael had moved to Marysville with his mother and an adult sister, Gina, and well, he didn't fit in with the "Go Vikings" crowd. He was from LA and told everyone that he had played in a rock band. He had chiseled features and long black hair, and all the jocks thought he was the illegitimate kid of some movie star. In class, he was smart enough that he could have easily won on Jeopardy. He was kind of a loner and seemed to prefer it that way. Sera noticed that Michael tended to sit back and study people more than he talked. It was on one of those occasions she noticed him silently observing her. Their gazes locked, and he smiled shyly at her.

sure his sister knew Sera crawled through his bedroom window practically every night. Gina was a music teacher by day and a bartender at night, so most of the time they had the whole house to themselves.

For dinner, she and Michael made her favorite, popcorn and fudge. At some point, talking turned to touching, and touching to exploring, and the next thing she knew, they were having sex. Nothing like the boys in Marysville, he was gentle and playful, as if sex was a little game he had personally invented. When he was ready to go, he yelled, "Giddy up!" That was her cue, and they hit their stride, pumping until they both reached a climactic orgasm. Oh, sweet Jesus, she felt dirty. She felt loved. And then the next morning, they would meet up and walked to school.

When Sera's dad died that year of complications from alcoholism, her family fell apart. Her mama had to work two jobs to make ends meet and simply didn't have time to comfort her. Her older brother got involved with drugs and ended up doing time. An older sister got pregnant and moved in with some guy that knocked her teeth out one night. Another sister just took off one day, and who the hell knows if she was even alive. But there was one person that stayed close to her throughout it all—Michael.

She loved his playful side and that he could always make her laugh. To her, he was like the moon in a starless night. But there were times, when he seemed preoccupied, and she didn't understand why. Then one night, she saw the dark side of his world.

She tiptoed to his bedroom window. She heard a woman's angry voice, even before she peeked inside. She saw his mother, towering over him. He was sitting on the edge of the bed. His mother grabbed him by the hair and jerked his head back so hard it looked like his neck would have snapped. She was screaming and shoving something in his face. "Eat it, Michael. I told you to eat it!"

Michael tried to turn away from her. "I hate peanut butter, and I'm not going to eat it!" She attempted to slap him across the face, but he blocked her hand.

Sera wanted to leap through the window and kick her. Suddenly, the woman hurled the sandwich across the room. "No supper for you. You can stay in here until you starve to death." Slamming the door behind her, she locked him in his room. Michael didn't move.

Silently, Sera easily hoisted herself up and slid through the window and went to him. "Michael, are you okay?"

When he didn't answer, she pulled him to his feet. "Let's get out of here. Come with me."

He nodded. "Where are we going?"

"Trust me." They both slid out the window and hit the ground. "I have a place I want to show you."

Michael was attempting to wipe the peanut butter off his face with his hand. "I do trust you, Sera."

They ran the two blocks back to her house. She helped him into her father's pickup truck. No one had driven it since his death, so she unofficially claimed it as hers. Within minutes, they were in a forest surrounded by trees. It was the middle of the night. She turned off the truck and motioned to him. "Follow me."

They went deeper into the woods and headed up a moonlit path to an open area with a small mound in the middle. Finally, she stopped. "Sit here and close your eyes." Cross-legged, she sat before him and took his hands. He followed her lead. They sat in silence for a few minutes before she spoke. "This is a sacred place. An Indian burial ground."

Michael pulled back a little. "Should we be here?"

"These are my elders. Part of my tribe. You are safe here with me." She squeezed his hands. "Tell me, what do you hear?"

"I don't hear anything."

"Listen closer. Listen to wind in the trees. What else?"

He focused harder. "I hear running water nearby and a bird, I think."

Sera pressed him. "What do you feel? Do you feel the wind in your face?"

Michael took a deep breath. "I feel that. I feel my heart pounding."

She took his hand and put it over her heart. "Feel my heart beating with you." Next, she put her hand on his chest. "Now, open your eyes. Look around you, Michael. What do you see?"

"I see you, Sera."

She smiled at him. "There is so much more, all around you."

Michael frowned. "You mean like spirits?"

"Spirit guides will come later. Let's start with finding your guardian angels." Sera pulled him to his feet. "I will teach you how to discover their messages to you."

"I don't understand. What is a guardian angel?"

"Your guardian angels are spiritual entities that have always been with you. You chose them even before you were born. They never leave you. They give you signs, sometimes in nature, sometimes in what you think is a coincidence. But you have to learn to be quiet and listen for them."

"Show me, Sera." Michael finally smiled at her.

She kissed his cheek, "I will teach you."

* * *

A few weeks later, Sera was about to go over to Michael's for the night when she heard sirens. Slipping into a pair of jeans, she hurried outside to see what was going on. She ran as fast as she could. There were two police cars parked in front of Michael's house. Michael was sitting on the front porch in the dark. It was a moonless night. He said, "You can't be here, Sera." His voice sounded muffled.

"Michael?" Sera started up the stairs.

Someone inside turned on the porch light.

"No. Just go. Now." Michael quickly lowered his head. But it was too late. In the light, she saw his face. It was a beaten, bloody mess. His clothes were torn and disheveled.

"Your mother did this to you?"

"I'm begging you. Get out of here and never come back." In the background, Sera heard yelling from inside the house. Two more police cars pulled up. She saw a look in his eyes that she had never seen before, and he calmly said one thing to her, *"Run, Sera run..."*

Michael watched her until he couldn't see her anymore. One of the cops that had just arrived sat down next to him and handed him a tissue.

"Thank you." Gingerly, he patted his swollen lip.

She put her hand on his shoulder and pointed to the squad car. "You're coming with me."

"What did I do wrong?" Michael looked scared.

She shook her head. "You didn't do anything wrong. I'm taking you to the emergency room, Michael. We need to make sure you're going to be all right."

"I don't want to go there. Just call my sister. If she thinks we need to go, she will take me."

"She has already been notified and is meeting us at the hospital." The officer paused. "Though I'd like to know, what caused this incident tonight?"

Michael looked down the street where Sera had fled into the night. "It doesn't matter now. She won't be back." He wiped away a tear. "I sent her away before she got hurt."

* * *

Later that night, Sera tried calling Michael, but there was no answer. She never saw Michael again. Sometimes she would walk by his house. There was a light on, but no sign of him. He had disappeared as mysteriously as he had arrived.

Chapter 1

Marysville, 2010

The taxi driver stepped out of the portable potty and glanced at his watch again: 2:30 a.m. "Damn, this better be worth one helluva tip." I mean, who flies into Yuba City airport at this hour? "Probably some self-important politician." But Marysville? The only event that ever takes place in this ghost town is the annual prune festival and that had come and gone like a bad case of diarrhea.

Well, whoever it was, wanted to be taken straight to the hospital. No stops, no tours of the city, just straight to the hospital. Oh yeah, and they requested a nonsmoking chauffeur. So where the hell was this VIP? "Damned jet was supposed to be here two hours ago." The last time a jet landed in these parts was because it got grounded in a lightning storm. Hell, it made front page news in the local newspaper.

No one important flew to Marysville on purpose. To even call this an airport was a stretch. The only thing that flew safely here was kid's kites. Pulling a pack of cigarettes from his shirt pocket, he muttered aloud to himself, *"Just one won't give you cancer."* Pulling his ball cap lower on his brow, he chuckled as sat down in his limousine, also known as a yellow taxi cab.

Faraway in the night, he could hear the jet's engine whistling even before he could see the landing lights. As the jet began its descent to the runway, he could see this was no ordinary bird. Hell, maybe the governor was coming to town. As the jet coasted to a stop, he could see an inscription on the side: *Touch & Go.* He waited until the jet came to a full stop before pulling onto the runway. He had been instructed to pull right up next to the jet to pick up these VIPs.

After about ten minutes, a man built like a major household appliance with a shock of blond hair and a scruffy beard, was coming his way. Trailing behind, was a smaller guy in an oversized trench coat, ratty jeans, and a lot of black hair.

The Refrigerator had a Southern drawl. "Ah, this is the limo we ordered?" He cradled a suitcase under each arm as if they were ladies' purses.

"At this hour, the only thing on the streets out here is burglars and bad women. Oh yeah, and maybe drug dealers." Both men silently turned and confronted him with deadpan expressions. The smaller man shoved his hands deep into the pocket of his Al Capone coat. The taxi driver prayed he wasn't pulling a gun on him. "Forget I said that last part. I wasn't thinking."

"We've got more stuff on board, if ya don't mind?"

The smaller man lingered behind, never taking his eyes off him.

"Sure, no problem, fella . . . sir." It might be a good idea to show some respect to the Big Guy. "Would love to see the inside of a bird like this."

"I'll get the rest myself. Just put everything in the trunk, please." Big Guy turned to his companion, "You sure this is what ya wanna do, buddy?"

"No." The smaller guy nodded yes.

The first bag was labeled as belonging to DJ Jansen. Turning over the tag on the other bag, he read the name: Michael Dolanski. Michael Dolanski. He'd heard that name before. Oh yeah. Marysville's only claim to fame had returned home. "Hey, I know who you are! You're that pop star, aren't ya? Michael . . ."

"You're mistaken, okay?"

Just then the Big Guy returned with more bags.

"Well, you're sure not the governor!" The taxi driver was obviously pleased with himself. "God, my daughter would do somersaults. Why, she'd kill me if . . ." Without thinking, he lit up a cigarette.

"I'm not whoever you think I am. Christ, put out that damned cigarette. Don't you read about secondhand smoke?"

"Oh hey, sorry. Wasn't thinking, I guess. I know—no smoking." Stamping out the offender, he opened the car door. "Lemme help you into the . . ."

"I'm quite capable of getting into a car without your help."

Big Guy turned to the driver. "Take us to the hospital. As far as you are concerned, I am the fucking governor, and this other guy, he's secretary of state."

The taxi driver distinctly heard the smaller guy chuckle, "Oh man, you did not just say that."

Chapter 2

Sunday was a typical autumn day in northern California, comfortably cool, bright skies, and only requiring a light sweater. After mass, Father Joe headed to the hospital to get organized for the following day. As his friend Anni often reminded him, organization was not one of his skill sets. As he crossed the street, he noticed a large group of kids, mostly girls, waving signs and dancing to music. Giving them a wide berth, he avoided the crowd and entered the hospital via a side door.

Unlocking his office door, he enjoyed his quiet office. As the hospital chaplain and resident counselor, he spent part of his time visiting patients and acting as a sort of unofficial therapist. Sitting down at his desk, he stared at the jumbled mess of papers and sticky notes. He picked up his phone and dialed the front desk. "It's Father di Blasio. What's going on in the parking lot?"

"Pop star, Michael Dolanski checked in late last night. Everyone is complaining about the noise and traffic."

"What brings him way up here?" Joe was looking for an ink pen that actually worked. "Has security been notified? What's his name again?"

"Security is on it. Michael . . ."

"Yeah, right. Security must be in camouflage in the bushes. I didn't see anyone over the age of sixteen. Spell the last name." He found a pen and scribbled the name on a sticky note. "Okay, thanks. I'm going to make rounds, but I have my cell with me."

* * *

For Father Joe, his work day always started on the surgical floor with a coffee break at Anni Cavatini's office. She was the nurse manager who handled everything related to surgery. Today, she would be going over tomorrow's surgical schedule and would most likely be there for at least another hour. He never needed to knock, he saw the door was ajar, and walked in, sitting down in a chair across the desk from her. He always said the same thing: "Missed you in church this morning."

And she always replied, "And you'll be missing me until God returns to earth."

"Actually, it's Jesus. Jesus is supposed to return, not God. Have you always been so negative about the church or just since I came here?"

Anni smiled. "Coffee's on. Help yourself. And no, you know I think all churches are full of self-serving hypocrites. It's just since my divorce, well, the Catholic Church doesn't like me any more than I like them."

"And you know the church has lightened up on its stance on divorce. C'mon, Anni . . ."

"Nope. Conversation over." But she was still smiling at him.

He liked looking at Anni. (She pronounced it Ah-nee). Anni: *as in an antiquated throwback to the 1960s, though she wasn't old enough to recall that decade. A time when everyone had hope and still believed peace had a chance.* Cavatini: *a delectable dish with a fine wine.* When she let her hair down, it hung like a black curtain to her waist.

When he first came to Marysville two years ago, he learned that one of his duties would be to serve as a chaplain, which was kind of like being a counselor, at the local hospital. Since he had never worked in a hospital before, Anni had introduced herself, and made it clear, she was his mentor for all things related to hospitals. Even though Anni was a registered nurse, she didn't provide direct patient care. Mostly, she managed a team of nurses, doctors and scheduled the surgeries. Since she was the boss, she could let him into the surgical suite to watch various surgeries from a safe distance, of course, and he often tagged along when she was covering the emergency room on weekends.

There was an assigned social worker to deal with families when tragedies occurred, but more often, it was Joe's job, as a minister, to handle the families when someone died. Like this one night a kid stole a motorcycle and was flying like a comet through the countryside. He probably never saw the cow standing in the middle of the road. His last words were probably, "Oh shit," and it was just that.

Joe and Anni had stood in the cold light of the autopsy room, staring at this sixteen-year-old kid that must now be made presentable so his family could come in to identify him. It was those kinds of moments that transcend all other thoughts, melting like hot candle wax, oozing into tiny crevices of your subconscious, into a secret place that only comes alive in nightmares.

"Hello over there . . . Joe?" Anni was waving a piece of paper at him. "Wake up. More coffee?"

Joe took the paper from her. "What's this?"

"Biopsy in the morning. It was just added to the schedule. Haven't met the musical star yet? Michael Dolanski?"

"I heard he is being guarded."

"No, that's his friend, DJ."

"No, I meant security . . . however I haven't seen any officers."

"Oh, they're at every door and elevator in the hospital, but they are plainclothes, so yes, undercover. We've even had kids trying to get admitted so they can get close to him."

"And we have him hidden where? The penthouse for VIPs that we don't have? Tell me, why Marysville? I'm missing a piece of the story, I think."

"I guess he grew up here. His sister still lives here. I think he was trying to avoid publicity." Anni pulled up the blinds and peeked at the growing crowd in the parking lot below her window. "So much for Plan A."

Joe scanned the paper in his hand. "Ah, man. Metastasis from testicular cancer? And he's some kind of a Greek god to all these girls? Where is the social worker for these issues?"

"She's on vacation. And it gets worse, his doctor is Martin Frobisher."

"I thought he retired or something last year. Didn't we all have a party and a cake for him?"

"That was his 110th birthday," Anni stated sarcastically. "He should have retired about two decades ago. The man shouldn't even have a license to practice. His daughter drives him everywhere because he can barely see." Anni chewed on the end of her pencil. "Go talk some sense into him. It's not too late for him to hop back onto that jet. I can cancel this procedure with one swipe of my pretty pink eraser."

Joe started to speak, but Anni interrupted. "I tried talking to him already."

"You struck out." It was more of a statement than a question. Outside, the crowd was growing larger and louder by the minute.

Chapter 3

Being born in Peoria, Illinois, was nothing to get too cranked about, especially in Joe's family. His mother repeatedly told the story to anyone that would listen that she had married late in life, and if God were to bless her with children, her firstborn would be raised to serve the Lord. Joseph was her first, last and only heir to the kingdom of God. Amen.

His father was a blue-collar factory worker. Back then, Caterpillar was the rock of Peoria. Everyone knew someone who worked there. After work, his dad could usually be found at a local bar with his buddies. Growing up, Joe saw so little of his father that he wasn't sure he would be able to point him out in a crowd.

By all standards, Joe was a good kid or, as he would later describe himself, "boring." Good grades, never in trouble, always did what he was told. As a child, he only played with friends his mother handpicked, was an altar boy, and sang in the choir. In high school, he insisted on joining the marching band. His mother preferred the orchestra, but for once his father intervened, and told his mom: "Let him play whatever he wants."

So Joe picked the drums. He loved marching in the parades and on the football field. Even though he wasn't big enough to play football, he at least felt like he was part of the game. He made new friends that his mother never met, and even tried pot for the first time at age fifteen. However, at home, it was a very different story.

His mother practically required strip searches every time he came home. She said he must keep himself clean and pure in order to enter the priesthood. While she didn't mind if he had girl *friends*, she wouldn't allow girlfriends. If he went out with a girl, she drilled him mercilessly for every detail, neurotically shadowing his every move. If he had his arms under the sheets at bedtime, she would order him to put his hands under his head, so she knew what he was up to.

Weekly, she conducted searches of his room for what she referred to as dirty magazines or telltale stains on his sheets. If he was in the shower for over ten minutes, she would pound on the door, demanding to know what was taking so long. Joe had often fantasized that the next time she pounded on the door, he would step out, stark naked. Secretly, he wished she would drop dead. But that's not what happened.

It was early January, and the trees were covered in crystallized glass from an icy fog that had crept in the night before. His father was driving him to visit a college a few hours away, which of course his mother had refused to consider. The roads had become a hockey rink, and the car started sliding. Back then, cars were not equipped with antilock brakes or even seatbelts. They had plunged over an embankment, and the car rolled over and over.

When he woke up, he was in a hospital. They told him he had been there for a week, in a coma. It was another week before they told him that his father had died in the accident. He never remembered crying or anything. He just knew that he couldn't move his legs. It was a month before he was finally able to come home. It would take an even longer time for all of his injuries to heal. He spent most of his senior year in a wheelchair and learning to walk again.

But the worst injury was the blame that his mother cast upon him. One day, it spilled out when she blurted out that if he had simply agreed to go to the seminary, none of this would have happened and his father would still be alive. His father's death should be a sign to serve God for the rest of his life. He never forgot her words. Even at her funeral several years later, he couldn't look at her without thinking that his mother died hating him for being such a disappointment to her.

But the worst and most humiliating moment in his life was in the summer right after graduation. Since his father's death, his mother had gotten a little part-time job because money was tight. He had the whole house to himself about three days a week. It was the closest he ever came to heaven.

There was this girl he had met in the band. She was pretty, popular and played the drums, too. They enjoyed practicing together. Joe decided they might like to practice something else together. Foreplay seemed to start out all right, but then he thought of his mother's reminder to him and went as flat as a balloon with a hole. It just lay there, flaccid and obedient to God. It was at that point, he decided to join the seminary.

Chapter 4

Anni easily sidestepped the incognito guards and knocked on Michael's door. DJ opened the door and summoned her inside. "Hey, how are you guys doing?" She tried to make it sound light and relaxed.

DJ was the band's drummer, and as it turns out, the pilot for *Touch & Go*. He was also Michael's best friend. Strategically placing himself between the bathroom door and Anni, he looked like he spent a lot of time in the gym. The clothes he wore accentuated every well-defined ripple. When he spoke, she was surprised at his deep Southern drawl. "He's in the bathroom. He's been throwing up again." He hesitated. "He vomits blood."

"Oh. I'll let the doctor know." Anni was clutching the consent papers in her fist. "I need to review these with him before tomorrow. He has to sign these papers before we can do the biopsy."

About then, the door opened and Michael stepped out, looking a bit more like kid caught in the rain than a star. His black hair, pulled back into a ponytail, made his face appear gaunt, and any color he had before had been apparently been flushed down the drain in the bathroom. His eyes locked onto her, and she noticed he had blood on his lips. "What do you need?" He sounded like someone who has been sick for a while and is tired of trying to pretend.

"I need to review the consent papers with you." Anni took him by the arm, "First, let's get you back to bed."

She was surprised when he pulled back from her. "I can walk. I got this far, didn't I?"

DJ was a motionless mountain. She was sure no one ever got past him or dared to try.

Anni held her breath, watching Michael as he weaved his way across the room and eased himself into a chair next to the window. He pulled back the blind and looked outside. There was a park across the street. A few children in strollers went by, a jogging couple and someone walking a dog.

Michael motioned her over. "Consent forms. I can also read."

Anni handed him the forms and sat down a few feet away. She glanced back to DJ, who was still playing statue in the corner of the room, now guarding the door to the hall. She could hear a clock ticking somewhere in the room. The TV and most of the lights were turned off. He looked up at her, and asked, "Risk of complications?"

Anni took a deep breath. "Yeah, let's go over those." She started down the list, when he put his hand in the air.

"Excuse me." Michael suddenly turned to DJ. "If you don't mind, I want to talk to her privately."

"Whatever." DJ cleared his throat and exited the room. The door gently closed behind him, and she turned on one light next to her patient.

Michael took a deep breath. "I will have this biopsy and nothing more. It says here, if further surgery is required, the doctor can proceed and that is not going to happen. I will leave this place just as much a man as when I walked through these doors. Got it, Ms. Cavatini?"

"We can change that line on the form to indicate your wishes." It was her turn to breathe. "Actually, you might want to consider a medical center that specializes in oncology treatment. This hospital is not equipped for . . ."

For the first time, Michael laughed. "What's the matter with all of you? Do you seriously think I'd come here for something like cancer? I don't have cancer. I'm only twenty-nine years old, for crissake. You medical people love a good drama. I know there is a lump, but I'm sure it's benign. DJ told you I was throwing up blood. I am not. I just cough until I puke. I think I caught some dumb virus on the road last summer. Antibiotics seemed to help for a while, but then my coughing came back.

"My sister wanted me to come home, so here I am. I'll be going home after the biopsy. I can't stay here. DJ also thinks he is clever and I don't know about the crowds outside, but I do. I guess he thinks I don't watch TV. He keeps it turned off when he's here, but at night, after he leaves, I turn it on, and I know the press is all over this shit. Everything I didn't want." He leaned back in his chair and closed his eyes. "Now, get me a pen, please. Let's get this over with."

But Anni heard nothing after *"I've been sick since last summer."*

Chapter 5

Clouds scudded across the early morning sky, threatening rain. Michael lay motionless, waiting for the presurgical sedative to kick in. DJ wasn't there. No one was there. His sister, Gina, would arrive at any time, which meant any semblance of peace and quiet would be over, as she tended to buzz around him like a hummingbird over a feeder. He took a long, deep breath and didn't cough. Good. He closed his eyes and decided to enjoy the drugs.

Suddenly, he realized he wasn't in his body anymore. Instead, he was floating somewhere near the ceiling. Sweet ride. When he woke up, it would all be over and he could get the out of this forsaken cellblock. For the first time in weeks, he could actually relax without feeling afraid. He was in the nice blue cloud of whatever the hell the drug was, and he liked not having to think for a while. He could stay here until this day was over and that would be just fine.

The past few weeks had been a series of being poked, prodded, and shoved into machines for photo ops that were never as fun as the ones with pretty girls in videos. All he really wanted was to go home. And by home, he didn't mean Marysville.

* * *

Seraphine was not on the list of approved visitors. But she was a massage therapist and worked at the hospital sometimes, so technically, she was cleared to be there. With the same animal stealth taught to her by her elders, she tiptoed to Michael's room. She already knew he was alone. She only had a few minutes and needed to make good use of it. When one of the guards turned his back, she slipped inside his room.

* * *

In the dim light, Michael thought he saw a woman, staring down at him. She seemed familiar, but far away and fuzzy. *Must be the drugs . . .*

The woman spoke his name, adding, "I wanted to see you."

The voice bounced like a pinball in his head. "Go away." *Did he say that or just think it?*

"You sent me away once . . ."

God, he couldn't make out the rest, but it suddenly occurred to him that he was hallucinating. Then she was gone.

A new voice interrupted, "It's time to go."

"Go where? Where are we going?" Michael tried to focus, but his brain felt like soup.

Anni was pushing him down the hall on a gurney, and Gina was holding his hand.

"I'm here, Michael." Gina squeezed his hand.

"But who was the other woman?" He blacked out.

* * *

Joe had forgotten his phone on his desk and when he retrieved it saw that he had gotten four text messages from Anni:

*** *Call me . . . where r u?*
*** *meet me in my office.*
*** *where in the hell are you?*
*** *fuck you, Joe!!!*

"I'm sorry, Anni." He found her in the hallway and pulled her into the nearest restroom.

"You didn't see him before surgery, did you?"
"I didn't get a chance."
"You promised me."
"I didn't promise anything." Joe threw his hands in the air. "You asked me to see him because you struck out. What did you want me to do? Go up there and tell him his doctor is really Mr. Magoo, and he should leave! Geez, Anni. Why don't I just fire myself while I'm at it?"

Anni had that determined look that he despised.

Joe gave her an exasperated sigh. "Why are you so bent about this guy? Dr. Frobisher..."

"... is worthless. Look at these reports." She shoved it into his face. "His PET scan results, alpha feto-protein levels, a CT scan of the lungs..."

"You might as well be speaking in Swahili." Joe was trying to make sense of it all, "Just give me a synopsis."

"He certainly has cancer. It has already spread to his lungs, possibly other locations, he is very sick." She paused. "He needs to be treated in a major university hospital, or he is going to die. It might already be too late."

"Dr. Frobisher should tell him." Joe was adamant. "It's certainly not my place."

"But you know he will downplay it. He needs an oncology specialist."

"Okay, I hear you." He put his arm around Anni, "I'll go up there when he returns from the biopsy. Get me some information. Referral options, something. I have to give him something."

"There are clinical trials. He can afford the best, I'm sure."

"What about his friend and family?"

"They don't know yet. I just pulled this report, so we know, and that's all for now."

"I'll go up in the morning."

"Today, please. After he wakes up."

"I hope I have enough time to pack my office tonight." Joe commented sarcastically. "That way, it will be quicker when I'm fired in the morning."

* * *

After Joe and Anni departed, Sera stepped out of the bathroom stall. She looked at herself in the mirror. *"You look sick."* She tried to apply some lip gloss, but her hands were shaking so hard, she dropped it. She spoke to herself, *"How did you get so sick? Michael, what's happened to you?"* She waited a few minutes, just make sure they were both long gone, then tiptoed out the door, leaving the lip gloss container as the only evidence she had ever been there. *"Somehow I have to help you, Michael."*

Chapter 6

Joe **probably stood outside** Michael's door for five minutes before he finally knocked. It was 6:00 p.m. Someone finally said, "*Come in.*" Once inside, he saw what he figured was Michael's bodyguard and a diminutive woman, much older than Michael. "Sorry to impose, I'm Father di Blasio, the hospital chaplain. I'd like to speak privately with Mr. Dolanski."

Both the man and woman stood up. The woman crossed her arms as if she were trying to hold herself together, "If you have anything to say, you can speak freely with all of us. I'm Gina, Michael's sister, and this is DJ, his best friend."

DJ extended his hand, "Nice to meet you. You are friends with the nurse, Anni, right?"

"Ah well, yes, we are friends." Joe wondered how he knew that, when DJ responded.

"I'm not psychic or anything. I've just seen you in the hallways and in her office, talking. I'm observant."

"So you are." If conversation was a sport, Joe figured he had dropped the ball. "I thought you were a bodyguard."

"Nah. I'm just the drummer in the band and Michael's friend." He had a laid-back style and casual smile.

Joe opted for small talk. "I played drums in high school. Not like you, of course." He might as well have said he loved the Three Stooges.

DJ nodded, still smiling, "Something in common. Who would have ever guessed."

Joe quickly turned to the woman. "You are?"

"Michael's sister." She still had her arms crossed. "And I have no idea why they sent you."

"Good point." Joe had to concede that. *He didn't know either.*

Up to now, Michael had been watching each person, as if he were watching an audition for roles in a play. Anni had described him as frail and weak. Right now, he looked like anything but weak. Finally he spoke. "So if they are sending a priest, can I assume this is bad news? Should we dispense with formality and just call hospice?"

"No, no . . . ," Joe explained. "But I imagine your physician will recommend a specialist. We don't have anything like that in Marysville. The closest would be Sacramento, but even then, you might want to find someone closer to home. Anni can research oncologists where you live."

Gina stood up and started to speak, when Michael pointed to the door. "Let me talk to the priest. Alone."

DJ and Gina filed out, but not without his sister casting a long hard glance toward Joe.

Michael was calm, but still the director of the scene playing out before him. "You owe it to me, to tell me first. I've been stuck by needles, shoved into machines, and today I had a biopsy to enjoy. Now you're using words like oncologists, Father um . . . ?"

"Just call me Joe." It felt like he had swallowed a large pill, and it was stuck in his throat.

"Joe, please sit down." Michael sounded like a father talking to a child, "Explain this to me, I'm a bit confused right now. Tell me what you know."

"It's not my place to tell you this," Joe began, "but the cancer may have metastasized to your lungs. That's why you are coughing up blood. It's also why you need an oncology specialist."

"So you are telling me I have cancer, and it's in my lungs? That's what you just said, right?" Michael's eyes were dark, unreadable.

Joe sat for a moment, wondering if this was him . . . "Yes, your doctor will confirm this."

In a matter of microseconds, Michael's expression ranged from stunned to horrified, then back to some semblance of feigned composure. "I need to talk with my family." He swallowed. "Unless you have something worse to tell me?" His composure looked close to cracking.

Joe stood to leave. "No. I'm sorry, Mr. Dolanski." Inside he was still pudding.

"I know you're trying for respectful, but seriously, please call me Michael." He had wrapped himself in a blanket, as if it would somehow protect him from whatever came next. "I do have a question for you."

Joe nodded. "I'll try to answer it."

"Why do you guys wear those white collars?"

"I'm sorry. What?"

"The white collar." He motioned to Joe's neck. "What does it signify? Is it symbolic?"

"I take it you're not Catholic?"

"Probably not a good time to tell you I'm not going to suddenly find Jesus, even if his face appears on a piece of toast tomorrow morning."

Joe took a deep breath. "It simply separates a priest from the secular world. That's all, really. Nothing mysterious."

"So, Father, what am I supposed to do next?" For a fleeting moment, Michael sounded vulnerable.

"Dr. Frobisher will review your test results and options for surgery, chemotherapy, and radiation."

"That sounds like a delightful smorgasbord of nausea, vomiting, and probably worse." Michael switched back to sounding shocked by everything. "People get diagnosed with cancer all the time. What are my odds, especially if the cancer has spread? This can't be happening to me. Couldn't there be some mistake? Some other explanation?"

"There are new drugs and treatments coming out all the time," said Joe.

"That's monetary comfort for the pharmaceutical companies, but I need more than that. Where do I even begin researching?" He was trembling under the blanket. "I'm a singer, for God sake, lung cancer? Are you serious?"

"Anni will pull some research for you. Actually, she's probably on the computer in her office right now."

"Send Dr. Frobisher in here. I need more information."

"Got it, sure. I'll send a message..."

"He doesn't know a text message from a smoke signal. Does he even have a cell phone?"

"Sending Anni a text... now." Joe hit the send button. "She can find anyone, even me. I'll come back tomorrow, if you like."

But Michael was staring at nothing, as if someone had accidentally hit the pause button and he was suddenly frozen in the moment. When Michael never answered, he headed straight for Anni's office. He didn't get very far when he was face to face with Michael's real bodyguard. Gina grabbed him by the arm. "Talk to me, now."

Chapter 7

When Gina came back into the room, she immediately parked herself next to Michael on the bed. "I've heard of an oncologist in San Francisco. He is supposed to be one of the best in the country. Tomorrow, I'll start making some calls. Don't worry. I'll take care of everything."

"You talked to Dr. Frobisher?"

"No, I spoke with that priest."

"Great. I thought that priests were sworn to secrecy. Let's pray he doesn't call a press conference."

"He didn't tell me anything, but I figured it out. DJ can go home in the morning. You will stay here with me until we get this figured out."

"The only reason I came here was because you insisted, and I want DJ to stay. Besides, I'm not staying past tomorrow. We have a recording session scheduled, and a guest appearance next week on . . ."

"Nothing more until we figure out the next step. We need more tests. Nothing is conclusive. This can't wait, Michael. If you do have cancer . . ."

"Oh, Gina, shut up." Michael was holding his head as if he had suddenly developed a massive migraine. "I don't know what Joe told you, but I'm telling you. It's conclusive. They have test results. Go home and get some rest. That's what I need right now. Actually, I think I want a Xanax."

"I'll get a nurse." She leapt to her feet.

"I'm serious." Michael pulled the covers up to his chin. "Please go home. We can talk tomorrow after we have all the facts. Right now, I just want to be alone."

Gina picked up her purse. "I'll send in that nurse with a pill." She kissed him on the cheek. "It will be okay, I'm sure of it, honey. I'm sure they caught it early."

"That nurse has a name: Anni. And I'm afraid nothing will ever be okay again." He turned out the light, leaving her standing in the dark.

Chapter 8

No one knows for sure what happened between Dr. Frobisher and Mr. Dolanski. DJ and Gina were not present. Anni had not arrived in her office yet, and Joe was stuck in a meeting at the church. This was a private chat between doctor and patient. Legend has it that someone threw a pitcher of water across the room. Bets were placed that it wasn't Frobisher. The hospital CEO met with Dolanski and his sister and told Anni to give them whatever they needed.

Later that day a memo, went out that stated Dr. Frobisher was no longer on staff. Usually, they added a little line that says something like: *"He decided to pursue other opportunities, and we wish him the best in his new endeavors."* But when you are older than crackers, well, what other opportunities are left? This time there was no party with a cake. He was just gone. Exit, stage left.

That afternoon, a surgeon from Sacramento arrived with an assistant carrying a portfolio full of important documents. Anni escorted them to Michael's room or, as it was now referred to, Michael's office. Michael had requested a table and turned it into a makeshift desk.

Both men looked like they had just sprinted in from a hit medical show on TV. The pro-surgeon, said his name was, "Dr. Panulapoddy, but everyone calls me, Dr. Poddy." His English was not as good as his hair. His assistant was a male nurse, "Rob." He said it like that wasn't his real name. Dr. Poddy was a Harvard alumnus and had worked in some very major clinics. Given his tan,

Rob probably spent a lot of time on cruise ships. Rob anticipated every move and laid out every piece of paper even before Dr. Poddy spoke. They had charts and graphs and percentages. They had clearly played this hand several times before.

Later that evening, Anni and Joe met at a quiet restaurant for pizza and beer. Anni told Joe that both men were kind, patient, and very thorough. "They handled Michael with the utmost respect and professionalism. Gina took notes, in case she had questions later. Dr. Poddy answered every question, and Rob gave her pamphlets, which made her feel important. DJ was quiet, expressionless. In the end, Michael agreed to surgery tomorrow, and after that, chemotherapy, but not to radiation yet. Michael plans to return home for treatment. Home, as it turns out, is Kapalua, Maui."

* * *

Anni offered to drive Joe home. "It looks like rain."

He waved her off. "I like walking. Clears my mind."

"See you in the morning." And with that, she was gone.

The streets were quiet. House lights in windows were clicking off as parents tucked their kids in for the night. A dog barked to be let back in, last pit stop of the night. Joe turned the corner that led either to his apartment or back toward the church.

On the other side of the street was a neighborhood playground. He walked over and sat down in a swing. Pushing with his foot, it moved a few feet. Reaching into his pocket, he pulled out his secret vice and lit a slender cigar. He had found these little treats years ago in the seminary. He didn't smoke often, but every now and then, it was just what he needed to help him think. He momentarily closed his eyes.

Sometimes he wondered about the lives of those families settling in together for the night. Husbands and wives, tangled under the sheets like grapevines clinging to stakes in a vineyard. The children would be in the next room, gently snoring. Sometimes he wondered what it would be like to make coffee for someone in the morning, plan vacations to Disneyland, and years later, they would be able to start and finish each other's sentences. The kids would grow up and have kids of their own, and it would be like starting all over again, when their own babies were little. They would share their lives together, embracing memories and laughs, holding hands until death took one of them.

Joe took a long draw and leaned back, peering into a star studded sky. "It's not going to rain." A shooting star sliced across the heavens, it hung on for an infinitesimal moment, and then disappeared. He walked back to the corner. Straight ahead and he would be home in less than ten minutes. If he went to the left and walked about five blocks, it would lead him to the church. Instead, he turned around started walking back where he came from. It would take him about a half hour to get there, but it was important. He knew what he had to do. There was something he needed to say.

Chapter 9

It was closing in on midnight. Michael was reading through all the information Dr. Poddy had given him one more time. Every time he came upon something he didn't quite understand, he reverted back to his laptop and began searching. There were a lot of medical terms and reports with scary sounding implications: Nonseminomas . . . fast spreading . . . alpha fetoprotein levels . . . Stage III . . . disease outside the retroperitoneum, involving nodal sites or viscera . . .

"What the hell does that mean? That doesn't sound good." He was reading aloud to himself, "Tumor markers include human chorionic gonadotropin and alpha-feta . . . there's that word again." Dr. Poddy said the cancer was Stage III. That meant it had metastasized or spread to others places. That explained the coughing up blood, fatigue, and weight loss. He had been so tired he couldn't eat. DJ would bring him something for lunch and ended up throwing it out.

Other than that, he never really felt sick. Back home, his doctor thought it was a virus. Antibiotics, rest, and fresh air would cure that, and for a while, that seemed to work but before long, it was back to that feeling of wading through deep water. The thought did occur to him that it was more than a virus. *Okay, Michael, stop it, focus.* He picked up the pamphlet on chemotherapy.

"Treatment with Cisplatin, Bleomycin, and Etoposide." He started typing again on his laptop. "Three to four cycles. Highly treatable, commonly curable. Good, good. Complete remission may be attainable in 10 to 25 percent of patients . . ." He slammed the laptop onto the table next to his bed and leaned back.

Are you fucking kidding me? He was relieved to be alone, that way no one could see his trembling hands. He was surprised by a soft knock on his door. Since it was too late for visitors, he figured it was another nurse doing rounds, as they seemed to be constantly monitoring stupid things like his blood pressure or if he was secretly bleeding to death under their careful watch. "Come in, I guess."

"The nurse said you were still awake." Joe was wearing jeans and a sweatshirt. "I couldn't sleep, either. I've been thinking about you."

"I've thrown better parties, but come on in." Michael looked studious in a green silk robe and dark-rimmed glasses. His hair was down tonight, falling in dark layers to his shoulders. He had softly chiseled features and dark watchful eyes that looked distrustfully at him in the same manner that Anni's Siamese cat looked whenever Joe walked into the room. Actually, Michael was built like a panther, lithe and lean. "Do you always make such late visitation calls?"

"When I think it's important, I do." Joe gestured at the heap of papers. "That's a lot to digest, especially tonight."

"Hmm . . ." Michael was watching him. "I hope you didn't come all the way over here to pray."

"I wouldn't be so presumptuous, Michael."

"If someone had told me a year ago that I'd be sitting in a hospital bed in Marysville, California, chatting it up with a priest, at midnight none the less, and that tomorrow I was going to have the worst kind of surgery a guy could have, I would have thought I was stuck in some god-awful reality TV show, and we need to find a way to get booted off the island really fast."

"I'd have to agree with you." Joe sat down. "Let's just say I'm here because I'm having empathy pain. What I wanted to say to you is that I understand what it's like to be scared of the future."

"Were you diagnosed with cancer?" Michael was suddenly alert.

"No, it all started with an accident."

"What happened?"

Joe took a deep breath and began telling Michael his story about the accident, his mother blaming him, and his struggle with his guilt. Michael looked thoughtful, listening attentively to every word. When Joe was finished, he said, "Michael, I felt emotionally crippled. I was so scared people would find out that I went into the priesthood, not because I was devout, but because I was too afraid to take a risk. I'm just telling you this, because I know what it's like to look at your future and hope no one knows the truth. I understand that emotion."

Michael softened. "You actually care about me. I'm impressed."

Joe nodded. "I'm not sure why I felt like I needed to tell you, but for some compelling reason, I knew it would mean something to you."

Michael gave him that half smile. "It meant a lot to me that you risked being vulnerable. That says something about your character. You're a good man, Joe. Please come back tomorrow. I'd like to talk more with you."

Chapter 10

Joe cleared his calendar in order to arrive early the next morning. Surgery was scheduled for 8:00 a.m. At 7:00 a.m., Gina had already been there for an hour. Anni was behind closed doors in a meeting with her staff. DJ was nowhere in sight.

The chapel was empty and quiet, except for a fountain gurgling in the atrium just outside the door. Joe knelt, crossed himself, and began to pray. Michael might not care, but it comforted him to say a prayer. He asked God for hope and healing, for guidance of the surgeon's hands, to ease the anxiety of the family and bring them peace. He also prayed for himself, for wisdom and direction. Somewhere in there, he saw Anni's face, and smiling, he asked God to watch over her. He continued his prayers for parishioners and specific problems in need of divine intervention and for those things beyond his power, like ending war and poverty. He wasn't sure how long he had been there, but he became aware that he was not alone. Turning, he looked to see who had sat down only a few feet away.

Gina wiped her eyes with a soggy tissue. "This seemed like a good place to wait. I hope I'm not imposing."

"No, no, of course not." Joe sat back on the pew. "Would you like some company?"

"Yes, I would." She smiled, a little. "I'm not Catholic though."

"There's a lot of that going around lately." Joe couldn't help but notice a small suitcase resting next to her. "I hope this doesn't mean you are moving in. I've had to stay over a few times, and the accommodations aren't great."

"This is what gave me comfort last night. Would you like to see what comforts me?"

"If you want to share, sure."

Carefully, she sat the case between them and released the latches. The air was perfumed with a soft hint of baby powder. Gingerly, she picked up a tiny bracelet. "This is the bracelet he wore in the hospital when he was born. It's blue, for a boy."

"Oh, thank you." He was surprised that she handed it to him.

"I took so many pictures. Here is the first picture I ever took of him, still in the nursery. And this." She picked up a tiny sleeper. "This is what he wore home. He was born almost a month early and only weighed four pounds. At first, I was scared to even hold him, let alone bathe him and feed him. He was like holding a doll."

"You couldn't have been very old yourself." Joe said, "Being able to help your mother with a premature baby, she must have trusted you or taught you well."

"Oh, I was almost seventeen." By now, she was thumbing through picture albums. "Wasn't he adorable? Look at all that black hair and those big brown eyes."

Joe smiled at the little guy smiling back at him in the pictures. She was right. He was . . . actually pretty. He looked closely at Gina. Fluffy brown curls, blue eyes, and to put it nicely, generous curves. The next thought was as close as he ever came to having Tourette syndrome. "Where are your parents? Why aren't they here now?"

"What?"

"Mother and father." Tourette's had given way to something even worse: stupidity.

"I know what parents are." Gina sniffed.

He now understood where Michael got his gift of sarcasm. "I mean, do they not live here?"

"Mother and Father are both deceased. I'm the only family he has left. Though there is an aunt that lives in Ohio." The words fell like someone rehearsing for what to say in a courtroom. They all died one day. End of story. Next question?

Actually, he did have another question. "Do you have pictures of your parents? I was wondering, does Michael favor his mother or father?"

She was quiet for a moment. "His father was Native American. He looks like his father."

"That explains his black hair and high cheekbones. So no family pictures?" He saw a photograph of two babies, lying beside each other. He picked up the picture. "Who's the other baby?"

"Oh, that's my aunt's baby."

"Ah, okay." He pressed one last time. "I'm kind of guessing you and Michael didn't have the same father?

"Yes, we have different fathers. He never met his father. His father left shortly after he was born." She sighed deeply. "Mother died several years ago. She was never a well person. I spent my entire life taking care of her. I should have been a psychiatrist. I was his mother and father."

She was holding a picture of herself and Michael. In the picture, Gina had her arm around him, and they were both smiling. He guessed Michael to be about six years old. Gina looked like a college girl with much darker waves framing her face and a very short skirt. She was pretty, and he realized they both had the same smile.

"Who took that picture?"

"If you're thinking it was our mother, you would be sadly mistaken. Mother couldn't find the bathroom, let alone a camera. It was just the two of us."

Joe frowned. "So you raised him?"

"Yes, I did the best that I could." She was still looking at that particular picture. "Just before this picture was taken, Michael had found a baby bird that had fallen from its nest to the ground. He carried the little bird back to the house, cradled in his hands. But when he got there, he showed it to our mom, and she started yelling at him and told him he had crushed it to death. He was devastated. She ordered him back outside and told him to bury it under the tree."

She seemed to be reliving the moment. "That's where I found him, crying. I helped him bury the bird and told him it wasn't his fault. He said when he picked it up, it was blinking and flapping its wings. So I explained that maybe birds with a broken wing just wanted to die. We buried it in a shoebox and had a funeral for the bird.

"Afterward, I took him for ice cream. But Michael didn't want the bird to be alone, so we had this picture. He stuck the picture in with bird. That night after he went to bed, I went back out and dug up the picture. If you look closely, you can see there is still dirt on the back." She put the picture back and picked up a picture of an older Michael, probably in his mid-teen years. He was holding a guitar.

"You know what I think," he said, "I think that even a bird with a broken wing can sing a splendid tune."

She smiled at him like the girl in that long-ago picture. "I don't want Michael to have a broken wing. He suffered enough as a child." She started to cry again. "Keep this picture for when you pray. I have many more like this." She pulled herself back together. "I'm going back upstairs to wait for him." She locked the suitcase, then added, "Thanks for listening. And I know I'm overprotective. I always have been, and it's probably going to get worse. Anyway, I'm going back upstairs. I want to be there when he wakes up."

He watched her make her way down the hall, toting her little suitcase of memories. That is when he realized he was still clinging to the blue baby bracelet. He started to go after her but changed his mind. Tucking it into his pocket, he made a mental note to give it to her next time he saw her. He spoke aloud to himself, *"I wonder what she meant about he has suffered enough?"*

* * *

Sitting alone on the other side of the chapel, Sera began her meditation. She believed that prayers cannot be seen, but can be felt and that feelings are the union of thought and emotion. She believed that our hearts have the strongest of all electrical fields and that compassion is the glue that holds everything in the universe together. In her culture, we are all only one particle separated from each another and can still reconnect like magnets, even after time and distance, we can influence the outcomes, connect the particles, and even heal each other because we believe we can. With that thought, she set about to reconnect with Michael.

Chapter 11

Outside the hospital, the crowd in the parking lot below continued to grow. Michael and DJ worked it out with the hospital to start a rumor that they had left town and no one knew where they had gone. *Touch & Go* was no longer parked at the airport. Gina looked at her watch: two hours. Surely, there would be some news soon. Reaching into her purse, she chewed another handful of antacids.

"Hey." DJ made an entrance and flopped into an oversized chair, dropping a large brown paper bag onto the floor.

"Where the hell have you been?" Gina demanded.

"Well Gina," he began, "I had a jet to hide, and since she's a pretty good sized girl, it wasn't all that easy to do. Right now she is tucked away in a cozy hangar in Sacramento. I spent the night in a hotel there, then rented a car and drove back here this morning. Michael knew where I was." He hesitated, "Speaking of Michael . . ."

"Nothing yet." She was pacing. "I'm getting nervous."

"It's not been that long, really . . . if you figure an hour for surgery and an hour in the recovery room. Not that I'm a doctor or anything, but that sounds about right to me."

She stopped pacing. "How did you get in here?"

"What do you mean by that?" He laughed slightly. "The usual way, I guess. I walked."

"No." She was staring out the window again, pointing her finger. "Past them. How did you do it? Did anybody see you?"

DJ sighed, leaning back in his chair. "I came in through the morgue as a dead guy. Then I rose from the dead, walked over to the freight elevator and came up here. It was prearranged with Anni. Satisfied?"

"I think you're lucky it worked."

"Maybe I went to secret agent school." DJ pointed to the bag on the floor. "I was in disguise. No one saw me, Gina."

They were interrupted by a knock on the door. Anni poked her head inside, "May I come in?"

DJ motioned her in with a wave of his hand. "Here's my partner in crime."

"Love the boots." Anni pointed toward his snakeskin boots. "Apparently, our plan worked, and you slipped into the hospital without any problems?"

"I'm getting pretty good at it."

Gina interrupted, "Did you just come in to chat with DJ about fashion, or do you have an update for us?"

Anni put on her professional face. "Your brother is out of surgery and in the recovery room. He came through everything well and should be back in his room in about an hour. Dr. Panulapoddy should be here shortly."

Gina sank into her chair, sighing deeply. "I just need to hear from the doctor."

As if on cue, Dr. Poddy walked in without fanfare. "We removed the tumors without any complications. In a few days, he should be able to travel and can go home. I don't expect any problems, but we will monitor him for any signs of bleeding or infection. He is on some strong medications for pain, and might be groggy today and tomorrow.

"After he recovers from surgery, we will start the chemotherapy as discussed. I know he said he doesn't want radiation, but that will be the best option for his lungs. Michael is probably going to react with a variety of emotions—denial, anger, sadness, even possibly depression. Be patient with him. Questions?"

Gina stared at nothing. "What is his prognosis?"

"He's young and strong, that's in his favor." Dr. Poddy was the kind that went straight to the point. "But I think we have a long road ahead, and sometimes it won't be an easy one. Of course, we're going to hit this cancer with everything we can. But right now, he's a very sick man."

Chapter 12

To Michael, it sounded like a low-pitched mantra: *OMMMMMM.*
"It's time to wake up. Michael . . . Michael . . . open your eyes . . ." He shook his head, no. Somewhere people were talking but there were no words . . .
"Wake up, open your eyes."
He tried, he really did. He saw a blur, softly screaming his name, *"Michael, Michael, Michael."* He blacked out. Under the waves of anesthesia, he tried to climb out, but was struck by a deep thudding pain that rendered him helpless. He wasn't sure if he spoke or merely thought the words: *Help me.* "Something for pain . . ." and he was gone again, pulled back into the undercurrent beneath the waves. He didn't see anyone or anything that was familiar. For the first time, he felt mind numbing fear, the kind where in dreams you are being chased by some faceless monster and you run as fast as you can, finally reaching safety and try to open the door, but it's stuck, and the monster is so close you can feel it's breathe on the back of your neck.
Suddenly, he had a sense of someone next to him, holding his hand. He tried to focus and hold on. It seemed there were two faces . . . then only one . . . he knew if he let go, he would go down, and this time he might not come back. *"Mom . . ."*
"It's Gina. I'm right here, honey."
"I don't feel so hot." With that, he vomited, then began so shaking violently he thought he was having a seizure.

The nurse explained it was a reaction to the anesthesia and not uncommon. She gave him an injection for nausea. He drifted again. But this time, he felt safe because he wasn't alone.

Chapter 13

Friday nights were reserved for Joe and Anni. Sometimes they went out for dinner; sometimes they just hung out at either Joe or Anni's place. It was part of their routine. Neither of them seemed to care if the other had to call off. Joe never thought of it as a date. In his mind, Anni was his best friend. He just loved being with her.

Tonight was Anni's turn to host. Since she was Italian, it meant any kind of pasta was her specialty. Even before he came through the door, he could smell the lasagna. Joe brought bread and wine. His specialty. Anni handed him two glasses.

"How was Michael when you left today?" said Joe.

"Sleeping off anesthesia. His sister was with him. She's something else."

"What does that mean?" Joe handed her a glass of chianti.

"It means that sometimes she is a lemon and other times she can be a peach. I never know which flavor I'm going to get when she's there."

Joe toyed with the bracelet in his pocket. "I think she doesn't know what to do. She seems like the type that is used to being in control. She has no control over this, and she is panicking."

"I don't think DJ likes her, either." Anni frowned. "I think he just tolerates her."

"Did you say either? Hmm . . . possibly. He seems pretty laid back in contrast to her." Joe took a sip of wine. "What do you know about DJ?"

"I've had an opportunity to chat a little bit with him. He said that he is like a big brother to Michael. They live in Maui. Oh, and he is actually a pilot. He flies that jet, *Touch & Go*." She finished preparing the salad and sat down across from him. "I think he comes from money."

"Well, I don't think either of them is hurting in that category." Joe paused. "In my opinion, DJ will be a key player once they return home. Unless Gina goes with them, which could happen, I guess. As far as I can tell, she doesn't have a job."

Anni laughed. "She doesn't need a job. Actually, I'm surprised she doesn't live in Maui. If I had a brother like Michael or DJ, that's where I'd settle down."

"In my opinion, I don't think Michael would allow it. He's too independent and likes to be in control. Haven't you caught on to that, Anni?"

Anni wrinkled her nose. "You're the one with a degree in psychology, what does that mean when someone feels the need to be in control?"

Joe shrugged. "Sometimes it just means they fear not being able to control their environment."

"I think it means they're afraid of being vulnerable, the fear of losing control."

Joe smiled. "Let's pick all of the above. You're probably overthinking it. Have some more wine."

The buzzer on the stove signaled dinner was ready. Anni sat there, staring into her glass as if an answer might bubble to the top, like in one of those eight balls with a floating answer. Finally, she spoke, "So, Joe, are you trying to tell me I'm controlling?"

"Nah." Joe laughed. "I'd be more direct than that." He stood up. "I'll get the lasagna before it burns."

* * *

When Joe awoke on a couch in Anni's darkened front room, he was momentarily disoriented. Anni was nowhere in sight and had probably gone to bed. Her cat was draped over the arm of a chair, staring at the dying embers in the fireplace. Slowly, he put on his shoes. Too many glasses of wine later, Anni had thrown him a blanket and told him to spend the night there. He needed to go home, get a shower, sober up, perform early morning mass, then go over to the hospital . . . world without end. Amen. Scribbling a fast note on a napkin to Anni, he tiptoed out the door. He heard the grandfather clock chime behind him and only then did he realize it was three o'clock in the morning.

Chapter 14

Outside, the fans had begun to trickle away, leaving behind *"We love you"* signs and a mountain of trash.

Inside, it seemed that Michael was never left alone. Gina hovered like the proverbial helicopter mom, nurses came and went, Dr. Poddy made a guest appearance, and DJ came later in the day, apparently not a morning person. Even though Anni was off duty since it was the weekend, she came in around lunch time to talk with Michael.

Anni considered Michael to be her patient, which meant she was personally responsible for his well-being while he was on the third floor. She thought about what Joe had said last night. If for one minute she was under the delusion she had any control, she quickly found out where she stood in the world of Dolanski. "I wanted to see how you're feeling today, Michael."

Michael was sitting up, sipping something his sister had brought in, since he was less than impressed with hospital fare. "Isn't Saturday a day off for you?"

"Well, yes, but I wanted to check in on you."

"What do you usually do on Saturday morning?"

Anni found herself blushing. "I'm usually teaching a yoga class."

"So you gave up yoga to check on me?"

Anni felt like she was being tested. "What you're going through is more important than an exercise class. I can schedule a make-up class. There are no do-overs for you."

43

Michael smiled, slightly. "We need to talk."

She sat down in a chair next to him, sensing she had passed a test.

He was direct. "I want you to come to Maui with me. I have no idea what to do next, and I need someone with expertise in the medical field. I'm asking you to be my personal nurse."

It felt like her entire world had suddenly collapsed beneath her, and she was swallowed into a black hole. "You want me to leave my job and home and be your nurse?"

"Well, I don't know if that is possible for you, so I'm asking, politely, I hope. You may have other obligations, and if that's the case, I'll understand. Family comes first. I get that. But if you could come, I'd be very grateful, I think I can trust you."

"I'll need to speak with my manager."

"If you recall, the hospital CEO said anything to keep me happy, and I've already discussed it with him." He smiled at her. "This would make me happy or at least feel better. I'll make it worth your time, financially. But I need an answer tomorrow, because I'm leaving in two days, and I want you to come with me."

Anni paused. "How do you know I'm not married?"

"You're not married." He closed in. "You don't wear a wedding ring and another nurse told me that you have dinner every Friday night with the priest."

She was silent for a moment. "You ran a background check on me, didn't you?"

"Don't be offended, Anni. You will be living in my home and managing my medications. I have to know I'm safe with you. I hope you understand. I didn't delve into your personal life. I just wanted to make sure you weren't a former druggie or on the FBI's most wanted list." He paused. "You are coming home with me. Yes? Please . . ."

Chapter 15

Sera waited for any opportunity, just to see him for a few minutes. Her only worry was that she would bump into Gina. So far, she had managed to stay off Gina's radar and intended to keep it that way if she could. She was never sure if Gina had liked her. It was almost five o'clock in the evening when she finally got her chance. DJ and Gina huddled at the end of the hallway, speaking in whispers. DJ nodded and gave Gina a quick hug, then they both departed, going their separate ways. There were no nurses in sight, all clear. She hurried across the hall and pushed open his door. "Oh my god . . ."

Michael was standing in the middle of the room, pushing his IV stand alongside of him with one hand, and clinging to the bedrail with the other. "Help me . . . I'm going to . . ."

Fall. She caught him before he hit the floor. "Ah, damn it," he said.

"What are you doing? Are you supposed to be up alone?" Sera eased him back onto the bed.

"I was going to the bathroom. All I wanted to do was wash my face and brush my teeth."

"I'm sure you don't have bathroom privileges yet, at least not by yourself."

"I didn't realize that was an earned privilege." He suddenly stopped. "Seraphine? Where . . . how . . . why?"

"First, let me help you to the bathroom."

"Never mind about the bathroom." He was blushing crimson. "How did you get in here?"

"I know how to get around in the hospital." She hoped it sounded halfway logical.

"Maybe it's the drugs, but I don't understand."

She sat down in a chair next to the bed. She was sure he could hear her heart pounding. "I needed to see you again. I've tried to reach you so many times."

"This has got to be the worst timing ever." Michael stammered. "I mean, what can I say? That night was one of the most embarrassing moments in my life. My mother had just beaten the hell out of me and was threatening that you were next. She found out about . . ." Michael looked close to fainting. ". . . that we were, you know, playing around. So Gina shipped me back to a . . . well, um . . . a private school. I couldn't contact you. And then, I guess, we just lost track of each other. Honestly, I missed you, too."

"I sent letters and birthday cards to your fan mail address."

"I never saw them, but we have people who review those for us, so I don't get to read them all. If I had seen something from you, I'd know who you are. There aren't many people with your name."

Sera reached into her pocket. "Anyway, I want you to have my e-mail address and cell phone number. You can trust me, Michael. I want to help you heal from cancer." Leaning over, she took the liberty of kissing him on his cheek. "I've never stopped thinking about you."

Michael stared at the piece of paper crumpled in his hand. He was trembling so hard, he couldn't even make out words. He could feel his blood pressure pulsing so hard that his ears were ringing. Light-headed, his lips and fingers felt tingly, and he was sure he was going to faint. At that moment, only one thought coursed through his brain. "How did you know about the cancer?"

"I overheard a conversation between two people on staff. But I can keep a secret, Michael. I've been keeping a decade worth of secrets for you."

"That's true, and we do have history." He reached for her hand. "All right. Come here, Sera."

She sat down next to him on the bed. He gently put her hand on his chest. "I do have cancer. Right here. In my lungs. I'm scared to death, Sera. I don't know what to do." He looked lost.

"What are your options?"

"Chemotherapy, and they want to do radiation, too, but I don't know."

"Will you be staying in Marysville for a while?"

He shook his head no. "I want to go home. As you know, I don't have nice memories of this town."

Sera frowned. "Oh, I do recall. Whatever happened to Claire?"

"I think someone drove her into the woods and a wolf ate her."

"I'm taking the Fifth Amendment on this one."

They both laughed.

"Ah, wishful thinking." Michael added, "Seriously though, she had a massive heart attack about 5 years ago. I didn't come back for the funeral, either." He paused. "You know, I hate to ask, but I really could use your help."

She was still smiling at the thought of Claire, bumbling around, singing hymns, and lost in the woods. "What do you need, Michael?"

He was blushing again. "I really need to go to the bathroom."

"Okay. C'mon." She helped ease him to his feet. "While we're in there, I'll help you brush your teeth and comb your hair, too."

"Thanks, Sera." He let her guide him across the room. "I'm not very good about asking for help."

She nodded in agreement. "When are you going home, Michael?"

"In the morning. DJ is flying us back to Maui. That's where I live now."

"You have a way of flying in and out of my life."

"I'll call you once I get settled." He did his best to give her a little hug. "I have your number now. Thank you for coming to visit me. It was nice to see you again and know you don't hate me."

"Why in the world would I hate you? It wasn't your fault."

"I shouldn't have put you in danger. That's all I meant."

"Well, if you had asked, I would have gladly taken her for a joy ride into the mountains."

He laughed. "I think I'll hold onto that visual."

After she helped him back to bed, she located his hairbrush and began fixing his hair. He sat quietly while she pampered him. It was one of those little nurturing things they used to do for each other when they were kids. There was something calming about having someone to do that for you.

Just then, his door opened, and Gina stepped into his room. She braked to a full stop. "Oh, I didn't realize . . ."

Michael smiled. "It's okay. You remember Seraphine, right?"

Gina had a tight smile. "Of course. I'll come back in a few minutes."

"I think I should be going, Michael." Sera patted his hand. "It was nice seeing you again."

Michael squeezed her hand. "Thank you for everything. Stay in touch."

"I'd like that." With that, she left.

Chapter 16

It was Sunday morning. Joe had finished celebrating mass and everyone had gone home. That is, everyone except one person: Anni was sitting in the last row. He had seen her come in late. She sat alone.

"So what brings you here?" He sat down next to her, loosening his collar. "Perhaps we should start with confession?"

She did that little snort, casting him a sidelong glance. "By the way, you do a nice job with mass. I always liked the sacristy bells at communion. Nice touch."

"Why didn't you come up for communion? I would have served you."

Anni smiled. "No offense, but I don't want anyone serving me."

"Yeah, that would be you all right." They sat in silence for a while. Anni looked like she had not slept the night before. "May I ask again, what's up?"

"I'm going to Maui with Michael. The CEO is still nervous about wanting to make sure the Dolanski family is satisfied. He was more than cooperative with letting me go, since this is what Michael has requested."

"Just like that and you're off to Maui? What about Gina? Why can't she go?"

"Michael wants a private duty nurse to arrange his cancer treatments and take care of him."

"Okay, I understand that part. What about DJ?" said Joe. "He lives there, too, right?"

"He's fine with whatever Michael wants." Anni patted his knee.

"I think you'd better get used to the 'whatever Michael wants' rule."

Anni nodded. "Oh, and you're off the hook. My neighbor is keeping my cat. I know you aren't a pet person."

"That's not true. It's just I've never had a pet before." He frowned. "Now that you've brought it up, I'm not sure why."

"Yeah well," she smiled. "Cats are intuitive. They know when someone doesn't like them."

"It's not that I don't like her." He gave in to an exasperated sigh. "This isn't about pets. You're leaving. How long do you think you'll be gone?"

"At least four months. I'll be there for the duration of his chemo and radiation treatments." Anni sighed. "I just wanted you to know that I hadn't been kidnapped or ran away with gypsies."

"I'm going to miss you. It's just this happened so fast. I mean, what am I going to do on Friday nights without you?"

"Ah, that's sweet." Anni gave him a quick hug. "Stop by around eight tonight. At the very least, you can help me finish off a couple bottles of wine. After all, this is aloha for a while."

Chapter 17

When Joe woke up the next morning, he briefly considered calling the chemical dependency unit at the hospital. Looking at the clock, he realized he had overslept by two hours. Damn. He needed coffee. He wondered why no one had bothered to call him. Then he realized, he had left his cell phone in the kitchen. Damn it. Somehow he made it from the shower to the car. Thankfully, there was a coffee shop on the way to the hospital. He wanted to see Michael one more time before they all left for Maui.

When he arrived, he was surprised to see the halls were empty. He easily navigated his way to Michael's room and lightly tapped on the door. When no one responded, he cracked the door and peeked inside. It was empty, except for a housekeeper who was either emptying the trash or pilfering through it for memorabilia. "You have got to be kidding."

The housekeeper looked surprised. "Hey, it's not like I'm stealing anything. It's America."

Marching across the room, Joe grabbed the trash bag out of his hands. "Yeah, I know. Land of the free, so this belongs to me now. That's how it's really done in America."

Turning, he ran down the stairs to his office because waiting for the elevator would have been insufferable. Fumbling for his keys, he managed to unlock the door to his office. He dialed Anni's cell phone. It went straight to voicemail.

Falling into his chair, he sent her a text: *Where R U?*
Anni: En route to Sacramento. Where R U?

> Joe: Trying to catch up. When did u leave M-ville?
> Anni: 30 min. Gina is driving us . . . slow.
> Joe: Good. Don't leave until I get there. Please.
> Anni: NP. traffic jam. M said ok.
> Joe: On my way . . . wait. Where at the airport?
> Anni: DJ will send directions when we get there. He has to do something with a flight plan?? He said u will b fine. C U there. B careful driving! xoxo

* * *

Gina gave them each a hug. "DJ, call me when you guys land. Michael tends to forget."

"As always." He motioned to Anni. "I need to board and get ready to fly. Take off in about thirty minutes. If you have anything left to load, do it now." Apparently, this was one area where he was in charge.

"Sure." Anni stepped forward. Turning to Gina, she said, "I promise to take good care of Michael."

"If I didn't think you were capable, you wouldn't be going."

"Right." Anni spoke through clenched teeth. Turning her attention back to Michael, "Ready?"

Michael nodded. "What happened to Joe? I wanted to say thank you. We have to board in the next ten minutes, or DJ will cause us bodily harm."

"He texted that he's here, probably parking." Anni wished she knew. He hadn't answered her last two texts. "Trust me. He'll be here any minute."

* * *

Anni saw him first, sprinting across the tarmac toward them. The thought occurred to her this was the first time she had ever seen him do anything aerobic. Something about this scene made her laugh, but mostly she was just happy he made it.

Gina followed her gaze. "Father di Blasio, I presume."

"Hey Anni," he arrived breathless. "I got lost. I'm so sorry."

"I'm glad you're here. Thank you for coming." They hugged each other. Over her shoulder, she noticed Michael watching them. Joe kissed her cheek. She was sure she saw Michael wink at her.

Joe turned to Michael, who was standing patiently by the car. "You're in good hands, Michael. I know you're not religious, but I'm going to send prayers, anyway."

Sometimes Michael had a way of looking at people as if he was studying a complex work of art. At the moment, he was scrutinizing Joe. Over the past week, he had time to ponder that look and came to following conclusion: Michael was always trying to figure out if it was safe to let his guard down.

"If it comforts you to know, I do have a spiritual side." Michael gave him a quick fist bump. "Thank you for putting up with me. I know I can be an ass-ache sometimes."

"I didn't view you that way. I saw someone put to a stress test that no one would want."

Michael smiled. "I hope I passed." He added, "If you'd like a vacation, Maui's pretty sick."

"Sick?"

Michael laughed. "That means sweet. It's nice. Anyway, you're always welcome." He looked at his cell phone and turned to Anni. "I'm getting a text from DJ. He's giving us five minutes. Until we land in Maui, he's our boss."

Anni nodded, turning one last time to Joe. "Stay in touch, okay?"

"I already miss you." For some reason, he suddenly felt misty. He was hugging Anni when he felt someone touch his arm.

Michael was next to him, smiling. "I'll take care of her. She's in good hands, too. Mine." Suddenly, Michael turned away and was hugging Gina. Then, he was off to board the jet.

Joe turned back to Anni. "I'm not sure how I feel about that last comment."

Anni laughed. "Have I ever told you that you remind me of Tom Hanks?"

"In which movie?"

"The funny ones." She kissed him one more time. "Gotta go or get left behind."

He watched as *Touch & Go* eased into a cloudless sky.

Gina kept her eyes to the sky until the jet was as tiny as a faraway star. "Thank you for everything."

"You're welcome." said Joe.

"I also want to thank you for humoring me that day in the chapel. I was kind of a hot mess."

"Oh, that reminds me," Joe reached into the pocket of his jacket. "This belongs to you." Turning it over in his hands, he noticed the name on the bracelet: *Baby boy Dolanski. Mother Gina Dolanski.* He couldn't stop himself from staring at her.

"Yes," she replied. "This belongs to me."

Chapter 18

Once airborne, Michael turned to Anni, smiling mischievously. "I say we go visit with the pilot."

"Are we allowed up there?"

"I'm practically his copilot. C'mon, let's go."

She followed Michael to the cockpit, where DJ sat comfortably, headphones on, talking to someone and navigating the Sabreliner jet as if he were driving a car down the freeway. He waved them in. "Perfect sky." Anni always felt a like she was going to fall off the edge of a skyscraper, peering into the vast horizon. "Oh my, I feel dizzy."

Michael touched her shoulder. "Are you all right?"

"Acrophobia. Fear of heights. I'm okay as long as I don't look out the window."

DJ glanced up but didn't say anything. He looked preoccupied. Michael put his arm around her, pulling her back from the window. "Let's sit in the back. We can visit. We've never really done that before."

Anni quickly learned that visit meant he asked questions, and she was supposed to answer them.

"So Anni," he settled in as if this were a job interview. It occurred to her that, in fact, maybe it was an interview. "Did you grow up in Marysville?"

"No, but I am an original California girl." She smiled. "How about you? Are you a native?"

He nodded. "Then how did you end up living in Marysville?"

"I met this guy in college and made the mistake of marrying him. His family lived near Marysville. So I ended up there."

"Ah . . . divorced?"

"Once was enough. I'll never put myself through that again." She wondered if that was too much information, so she added. "What I meant to say was if I ever decided to marry again, I would want it to be forever." She tried again to move the subject off her and back to Michael. "Have you ever been married, Michael?"

"No, I came this close once." He held his fingers close to demonstrate an inch. "But I agree with you. If you're going to take the plunge, you'd better make sure you're not sleeping with a shark."

"Was she a shark?" She thought the conversation had finally turned away from her and focused on him. Wrong again.

He chuckled. "I'm sure sharks come in both sexes, but Gloria Stuart was more of a fisher for rich men. Anyway, where is your family today? Are they still living in California?"

She paused. Actually, she totally froze.

"I'm sorry. Was that a bad question?" Michael was intently watching her reaction. "I was just trying to get to know you. You don't have to answer. I meant this to be a conversation, not an interrogation."

"It's okay. I was raised in a series of foster homes. I always hoped someday I'd get adopted, but that never happened. I always wanted a real family."

"Oh, Anni," His face softened. "It's so hard to trust when you've been hurt so deeply. Sometimes it's just easier to keep that wall around you for protection."

"Hmmm . . . that comment sounds like someone who's been there." She smiled. "I'm okay, really. Joe is my closest friend, and I feel safe with him."

"Because he's a priest?"

"No, of course not, because he's kind and caring. But what's your story? I shared, so I think you owe me something back."

"Fair enough." He nodded. "When I was born, I guess my father took one look at me and decided it was better to cut his losses and leave. Unfortunately, my mother spent most of her time in mental hospitals, so I was raised by Gina. That's why she is so protective. When my mother was at home, she would stop taking her medicine and become psychotic. She could hit the trifecta on being verbally, emotionally, and physically abusive when she was in that state of mind. Actually, I got pretty sick of being her human bowling ball. Most of my childhood was spent getting shuttled off to various places, too. Finally, I ended up on a ranch in Texas. Actually, that's where I met DJ and his family."

"Did you resent being sent away?"

"I wasn't happy about it. I don't know your situation, but I do know what it feels like to never know what's next. Sometimes it was tough. Even though I knew Gina loved me, I wanted to be at home. Unfortunately, it was impossible, and I couldn't have friends or a normal life, whatever that might be. So I guess I became kind of a loner."

"My mother died from an asthma attack when I was about three years old. I have some memories of her. She spoke fluent Italian. She is the person that pronounced my name like it was spelled with an H. Ah-nee. I kept it that way. Her family still lives in Italy, but I've never met any of them. My father was in prison. Actually, I've heard he was with the mob or something. As far as I know, as a child, I never met him. There was no one in the family who could take me in, so that's how I ended up in foster care." Anni sighed.

"It's been a long time since I told that story to anyone. Actually, the last person was Joe. Some of the families were nice, some I think took in kids for financial reasons, and I was just a commodity to them. At times, I felt like the live-in maid and babysitter for other kids. No wonder I grew up to be a nurse. The proverbial caretaker."

"Well, I don't think we turned out too bad, Anni." Michael sat back. "We're both successful in our own right."

"It helps me to understand you a little better. Thank you for sharing, Michael."

He blushed. "Don't thank me yet. Let's see if you still like me three months from now."

Chapter 19

He hadn't done anything like this since he was a teenager. But for some unexplainable reason it seemed logical, almost a compulsion, that had to be done. And that's how Joe found himself standing in the music aisle at Wal-Mart.

"Can I help you find something, Father?" The boy went to mass with his family every week. Joe gave him communion. "I think you may have wanted the spiritual section. There's not a lot but we have some Christian music and, of course, oldies."

That's when Joe realized he was wearing his white collar. "No, I'm exactly where I want to be." He took a deep breath. "I want Michael Dolanski. I mean I want his music. He has a CD, right?"

"Well sure," the boy half-smiled, "I think he has four now. But . . . um, I don't know how to say this, but the lyrics are under sexually explicit. He's kind of like a Jamaican version of Jagger. Wouldn't you prefer something a little tamer? You know, the singing tenors, or maybe a musical?"

If there was any plausible way he could pull off a disappearing act, this would have been the moment. "No. That's what I came for. Michael Dolanski."

The boy smiled. "Alrighty then."

"Just tell me where I can find him?"

"Yeah, well . . . like which CD do you want?"

"All of them."

"Wow, dude." The kid high-fived him. "You go, Father. I mean who knew you priests . . ."

"It's not what you think. This is educational, research."

"Oh yeah, sure, I get it. I can keep a secret. Whatever."

"Seriously . . ."

"Dead serious. Hey, you might want to go online. He has some great videos. And you can consider this a confession, but some of those girls . . . oh man . . ."

"All right. Let's end this conversation, okay? Research. Nothing more."

"I'm all about higher education." He smiled. "Is there anything else I can help you with tonight?"

"Yes, I need a CD player or something. I don't have any way to listen to this."

"Oh, hey, I'll get you set up. No problem."

The kid made him feel like he had gone into the store and asked for porn. "Well, just remember, I'm your hookup. If you need anything else, you're good with me." He placed his hand over his mouth. "I saw nothing. Never saw you here."

Joe sighed. "Next time cover your eyes, not your mouth." The kid piled everything into his cart. "I think I'll just go home."

"Have a really nice evening, Father." He winked. "See you at mass."

Hurriedly paying for everything, he was finally in the privacy of his car and unwrapped the first CD with trembling hands. He popped it into the CD player in his car. Smiling to himself, he listened to the lyrics. "Just exactly what I needed." He couldn't wait to get home. After all, he had bought all of Michael's music and had already viewed all the videos.

Chapter 20

Anni gazed out of a wall of glass that reached from the floor to the ceiling. She took in the panoramic view of a perfect blue ocean that vanished into a golden horizon. From her view, the world seemed endless. There wasn't a cloud in the sky. Even though they were nestled away in an alcove, she could hear the waves rolling rhythmically, the eternal song of the ocean. Later, she learned they had their own private beach area. The scent of flowers wafted in the air: Tropical breezes caressed her face. Only one word came to mind: "Paradise."

DJ walked up beside her and smiled. "That's why we live here. Beauty and peace."

Anni breathed in every molecule of this new world. "Did you choose this place?"

"Nah. This is Michael's dream. It's his home." He laughed. "I grew up on a ranch in Texas. So technically I live in two places."

"Where is Michael?" Anni frowned. "He disappeared after we arrived."

"He's probably at the pool. He can spend hours there. Sometimes he sleeps in the hammock out there."

As he led her through their home, she tried to take it all in, then realized it would be like trying to see everything in one tour of a museum. To sum it up, it was a study in light and space. Immaculate and unpretentious, every turn was a balanced mixture of casual elegance.

The entire first floor was one large area that included the kitchen, dining area and formal living space. The kitchen had rich inland wood recessed ceilings and Brazilian cherry cabinets. The main area was more comfortable, boasting cathedral ceilings and skylights. Every room had ceiling fans that created soft breezes. Tropical trees were in huge pots and gave the feeling of almost living outdoors.

The interior was mixture of textures and colors. Windows filled entire walls so that there was always a breathtaking view at every turn. At the touch of a button, light grey shades appeared to float into place, assuring privacy. The floors were soft grey travertine, with accent rugs that added splashes of color. The furnishings were minimalist and functional. Bamboo sofas with plush cushions and rattan chairs were dotted with bright primary colored pillows. From what she could tell, there wasn't a bad seat in the entire place. On one side of the room was a fireplace with built in shelving lined with pictures and trophies, a testament to their successes.

DJ touched another button and one entire wall of windows glided open to the pool area, which really seemed like an extension of the house rather than a separate space. There were more sofas and lounging chairs, another outdoor kitchen with tables and chairs set up like an outdoor café. The pool was built in a manner that looked like you could simply fall off the edge of the world.

Later, she learned it was called a zero entry pool, which meant you could simply walk into it. There were inlaid fire pits at both ends of the pool and in one corner, a bar, which was a shady cabana. If you looked in one direction, you could see the ocean, but if you turned around, there were mountains. Quite simply, it was a plush paradise surrounded by lush tropical plants and total privacy.

"No Jacuzzi?" she asked.

DJ smiled. "There are three. But that's up there." He pointed to the roof. "There are private lanais where you can sit and look at the stars all night if you desire. No one can see you there. The perfect place for peace or playtime."

"I can't wait to see the rest of this mansion."

DJ frowned. "I never thought of it as a mansion. It's just our home. When we moved here, Michael hired a professional decorator. He pretty much gutted the place and started over. Michael had some very particular ideas, like the waterfall showers and closets that have rotating racks, so he can find anything at the touch of a button. Everything in this place is digital. I think he perfected the art of being able to do anything without having to move."

"Where will I be staying?"

"I believe you will be in the guest room that is usually designated for Gina. Once you get settled in, you can explore on your own. Michael and I are on the second floor. The guest rooms are in the loft area, third floor. You can get there by the spiral staircase or the elevator."

"Unfuckingbelievable. Do I have a lanai and Jacuzzi?"

DJ smiled. "Of course, you do. I think you will find the accommodations to your liking."

"Right now, I feel like a princess instead of a nurse."

"Let's go find Michael."

* * *

Michael was in the cabana, mixing drinks. He was wearing khaki shorts and a ponytail.

"Hey, Michael," DJ waved.

He waved back. "Anni, did DJ show you to your room?"

"Ah no, not yet." Anni was still attempting to take it all in. "How do you manage all of this?"

"It does take a lot of maintenance, so don't be surprised to see people wandering around during the day, or in other words, don't sunbathe naked by the pool." Michael was pouring them each a drink. "Let's see, the housekeeper is here for at least a few hours every day, except Sunday. We have a chef that comes in about three times a week, so you can let him know if you have any special dietary orders. Then, there is the landscape guy who tends all the plants and the pool company. A personal trainer comes in, but I'm not sure how often, since he is employed by DJ. A massage therapist shows up at least weekly for me, more often if I need her. I don't know. DJ, am I missing anyone?"

"Just don't leave the property without entering the security code, otherwise you will set off the alarms and piss off the local police."

"Got it. I think." Anni hesitated. "So what do you want me to do?"

"For now," said Michael, as he smiled, "your job is to keep Gina from coming here. We'll figure out the rest later."

Chapter 21

Joe's desk looked like the floor of the New York Stock Exchange. Looking down, he saw the picture that Gina had given to him of Michael. He smiled back at him. It had only been a week since they had all left. But it seemed like a month.

Gingerly, he toyed with his cell phone. He told himself that if Anni had needed anything, she would have called him. He laid it back down. Maybe they were all too busy to call. Staring at the phone, he willed it to ring. When it didn't, he picked it back up again and went to his favorites list. Of course Anni's number came up first. What time was it in Hawaii? At the very least he could leave a message. Now that he thought about it, he was surprised she hadn't called him. Perhaps Michael wasn't doing well. Maybe that kept her occupied. He stood up, watching the phone as if at any moment it might do something magical.

"Oh, for heaven's sake, just call her." He hit her number and waited. It rang three times, and he waited for it to go to voicemail when a man answered.

"Aloha."

"I'm sorry. I must have the wrong number." Frowning, he looked at his phone and saw Anni's picture.

"Isn't this Father Joe?"

"Who is this?" Joe demanded.

The person on the other end laughed. "Michael Dolanski."

"Michael!" Joe broke into a wide grin. "Why are you answering Anni's phone? Where is Anni?"

"Let's just say she surrendered her phone for a while. She's a tenacious girl, that one. Very dedicated to whatever she puts her mind to."

"I knew she would be helpful to you. She's a wonderful nurse."

"I wouldn't know much about that. But she makes sure that I get my daily exercise by walking with her every morning and evening on the beach. She makes our chef prepare healthy meals and yesterday supervised the guy who came to clean the pool. Anni makes friends with everyone, even the gardener and he never talks to anyone because he doesn't know any English. I'll bet you miss her. I may have to find a way to keep that cute little pony in my stable."

Joe frowned, "So where is she trotting around right now?"

"Right now she is flat on her back." It sounded like he put the phone on speaker. "Not more than ten feet away from me, poolside, making sure my massage therapist has good technique." He shouted to her, "Anni, my dear, Joe sends his love."

"This I'd have to see for myself."

Michael was back on the phone. "It can be arranged."

"Oh no, I couldn't."

"Of course, you can. You can drive to Sacramento. I've seen you do it." Michael paused. "I'll have boarding passes waiting. You can fly directly into Maui. We will pick you up at the airport, and the next thing you know, you're on vacation in paradise."

"I'd love to, but . . ."

Michael's tone dropped. "You have to come soon."

"Are you okay?"

"I'm trying to rest and recuperate. But you have to save me from this girl. Someone else needs to go on these aerobic death marches with her."

"Where's DJ?"

"At the moment, he's back home in Texas. In the meantime, I'm stuck on an island with . . ."

"Anni Cavatini." He was still smiling.

"Save me, Joe."

Chapter 22

Michael wandered into the kitchen and decided to whip up a protein shake. It wasn't that he was feeling particularly hungry, but that everyone should take in something life-sustaining now and then, and since he hadn't bothered with that since yesterday morning, maybe it was time. Hitting the remote, he opted to watch a little TV and catch up on the world news.

"Heavy thunderstorms continue to batter the eastern states. Meanwhile on the western side of the country, it is wedding bells for Gloria Stuart and Nick Paradise. Details after this message . . ."

Michael poured his drink into a frosty mug. The commercial ended and Michael turned up the volume. *"Nick Paradise, lead singer for the heavy metal band Eclipse was spotted in London this week with model Gloria Stuart. When asked to comment, neither would reveal a firm date,* but Gloria added, *'We're in love, and my daughter loves Nick, too. He will make a wonderful father to her.'"*

Michael stared at the screen. Nick, Gloria, and the little girl smiled back at him. His face was granite. "No way is that drug addict going to raise my little girl."

* * *

When Michael decided to break up with Gloria, certain considerations needed to be addressed in regard to his infant daughter. Michael turned to DJ and his family for domestic advice. Since DJ had nannies, he knew how to go about getting one after Rose was born.

Several interviews were set up, attorneys consulted and background checks initiated. Part of the contractual agreement between him and Gloria was that if he was paying for everything, he could select her caregivers and they reported directly to Michael. They could have shared custody of Rose, but with the understanding that Rose would live with her mother.

However, any changes in residence, schools or anything related to the child's health must be agreed upon, in writing, with Michael. Plus, he had the right to visit her whenever he wanted, though he was supposed to notify Gloria at least twenty-four hours in advance, which rarely happened, because if he did, she often skipped out with Rose, which meant he had made a trip for nothing. Therefore, Michael added a stipulation that if that happened two times in a row, they would go back to court. Gloria quieted down and stopped making that an issue. After careful consideration, Michael chose an experienced woman named Emily.

Emily was in her mid-thirties, warm and sweet as a Southern pecan pie, where she had been employed by the Jansen family for the past five years. As it were, DJ had a sister, who was married with two children and lived in one of the wings on the family ranch, or as they called it, the compound, outside of Plano, Texas. Since she and her husband had decided to move to Europe for a few years, in order to expand one of their enterprises, they didn't need two nannies. So Michael hired Emily.

Emily's contract was exclusively with Michael. Gloria wasn't aware, but Emily was required to call Michael every week with an update on Rose. Likewise, there were times when Michael was in LA on business and met up with Emily, so he could secretly visit with his daughter. These brief encounters were not relayed back to Gloria, and for now, they could get away with that, since Rose wasn't tattling back to her mother. Unofficially, the agreement included that Emily would be a watchful eye for what was going on in Gloria's world. Any indiscretions would be reported back to yours truly.

Reaching for his phone, he dialed Emily. "Did we miss something? I don't like surprises. Explain to me how this was missed."

Chapter 23

Over the next few weeks, Anni began to settle into the rhythm of a daily routine. First stop was checking to see if Michael was awake. In the beginning, he had seemed amiable to walking on the beach with her. But now, there was a touch of moodiness about him. It was usually around eleven o'clock when he finally surfaced, and his first order of the day was for coconut coffee.

"You missed our walk." Anni started.

"I didn't miss it at all."

"I'm starting to realize you are not a morning person."

Count Dracula responded, "I'm more creative at night. That's when I work."

"But I thought you told me you wanted fresh air and exercise." Anni hesitated. "You're the one that said to push you."

He gave her a look of exasperation. "Push me? Good luck with that."

"Okay, okay," she retreated, "how about some breakfast?" He turned away, ambling onto a lanai that overlooked the ocean, mumbling under his breath. "Oh my god, not another mother."

She made another attempt. "Maybe just some toast and peanut butter?"

"I detest peanut butter."

"That explains why I can't find any in the house." She tried one last time. "What do you like?"

"Coffee. Do we have any of that?"

"I'll make some." And that was how each day began.

After three mornings in a row, she gave up and let him win, which seemed to be a better option than having Dracula rip out a jugular vein every morning. Besides, there was still the evening walk, which he seemed half-willing to entertain.

Her next task was making calls and getting his chemo and radiation set up. So far, nothing was working out. Finally, she was forced to go back to Michael. He was in his studio. "I'm having trouble getting everything set up in Honolulu. Would you consider going back to California, say Los Angeles or even Sacramento where Dr. Poddy could monitor you?"

"Make it work, Anni."

"Honolulu can't get you scheduled for another three to four weeks."

"Is this an urgent matter?"

"Your chemotherapy?" Anni stammered. "Honestly, I am not sure how to respond to that."

Michael didn't respond. Idly thumbing through his mail, he seemed transfixed with one letter that had arrived certified yesterday. Finally, he spoke. "You have plenty of time to figure it out. I'd prefer to stay here, have you tried the Maui Memorial Medical Center?"

"I wasn't aware there was a medical center here."

"Call and tell them it's for me. I think they can handle this." He stood. "I'll be leaving next week."

"You're leaving? Where are you going?"

He looked over his glasses at her. "I have a two-year-old daughter in Malibu. I try to see her every month. I'm past due to pay her a visit. I want to spend some time with my little girl."

"So what do you want to do this week? I could teach you yoga, or we could make some peanut butter cookies . . ." Her eyes sparkled with light.

He laughed. "Oh Anni, we're in Maui. Let's go play."

Chapter 24

Gloria pushed white-framed sunglasses onto her nose and cranked up some music on the CD player. Pressing the accelerator to the floor, she let the wind whip her golden tresses into loose tangles. Smiling, she thought back on the press conference. It had gone viral; by now, the news was out.

All she needed to do now was plan her wedding. It would be more than a wedding, it would be an event. Something she had wanted with the one and only Mr. Fucking Wonderful Dolanski. But he never seemed to get around to the marrying part. It always seemed he was too busy: busy touring, busy in the recording studio, and as she found out later, busy with lots of other girls.

When she announced she was pregnant, he acted as if she had just told him she had contracted the Ebola virus. To his credit, he stuck around, and after the baby was born, a little girl, they moved in together at her beach house in Malibu. That lasted about a year before he was busy again. This time, she kicked him out.

Six months later, Michael had the number one hit of the year and was voted best new male vocalist. Cha-ching. Michael had promised to take good care of her and baby Rose. Financially, it was a promise that he kept, but as a father, he made cameo appearances. While she visualized him coming back so they could be a family, he moved farther away to Maui.

Then one day, she was chosen as a model in a video for singer Nick Paradise, and before the day was over, they had fallen in lust. Nick knew the magic word: family. She knew another word: yes.

After they were married, Nick wanted to adopt Rose as his own daughter. That was going to be the tricky part. Michael was going to go Chernobyl.

Glancing at her watch, she realized she was going to be late for her facial at the spa. Bounding two steps at a time, she approached the desk, where a young girl was sitting. "I have a standing appointment."

"I'm sorry. You are . . ."

"Gloria. Obviously you're new here."

"Gloria. G-l-o-r-i-a." She spelled out her name, enunciating each letter as she scanned the notebook for her name. "Yeah, here you are."

Her cell phone rang. She scanned her text messages.

***Spending afternoon with my daughter. M

"Cancel my appointment. I have to go home." She texted him back.

***Call next time, jerk.

Chapter 25

"**Hey dolly, how's daddy's favorite girl?** Look at you." He fluffed her blonde feathers. "You're getting bigger every day. I brought you a present. Let's see what it is, okay?" He handed her the wrapped box.

Sitting it on the floor in front of her, she tried for a minute, then did her version of sign language for help. Grabbing her own little arm, she waved it at him. "Help, help."

He smiled, pulling her onto his lap. "Okay. I'll help you." Inside was a doll from a TV show he had heard all kids her age liked. He had researched it en route to Malibu. "You like her? I hear she swims with her friends in an underwater world."

Clapping her hands, she threw him a big sloppy kiss, giggling.

Michael laughed. "I guess that means yes. So what do you want to do? Play some more or walk down to the beach for some ice cream?"

"Yes cream."

Scooping her up, he kissed her fluffy little head. "Sounds good. Then we can come back and play some more."

"You're not going anywhere with my daughter." Gloria surged into the room with the intensity of a tsunami. "You're supposed to call first."

"Our daughter, Gloria. Do you have a memory problem?" Rose was clinging onto him like a baby monkey. The floor was cluttered with dolls and toys. "That means I can have quality time with my daughter." Giggling, Rose wrapped her arms around his neck. "Dadda."

Michael smiled. "Like it or not, that's me, Gloria."

"Money doesn't make you a father."

"Custody doesn't make you a mother. We have shared custody, so I have rights to her. Do we need to review the rules again?"

Gloria smiled insincerely. "I guess you've heard I'm marrying Nick."

"You were foolish enough to hold a press conference, then serve me with legal documents, stating he wants to adopt my daughter. My attorney has already prepared a motion for a change of guardianship." He sat Rose down. "Go play with Emily, doll baby. I need to have an adult chat with your mommy."

"You never wanted a family," she snapped.

"I wasn't ready for a family, Gloria. Our relationship wasn't exclusive, and you knew that. You said you were using birth control, which was apparently a lie. You set a trap, and it didn't work, did it? Then you gave me an ultimatum. As you may recall, I'm not fond of ultimatums. But Nick Paradise? Why are you lowering your standards? There may even be a law against submitting a child to that sadomasochistic junkie. I'll have my attorney check out the buzz on that."

"Don't do this to me. I'm her mother." She was close to tears. "I loved you. But you always choose money and fame first. How can I compete with that?"

"I'm her father. Paternity tests confirmed that. You think it will be different with Nick? You're just arm candy. He's on the road even more than me." Michael lowered his voice. "I've already hired a live-in nurse who will care for her. You can have Nick. I really don't care. But Rose will . . ."

"You hired a nurse? You were just in the hospital. Why?"

"I caught a virus on tour." He was matter-of-fact. "I am fully capable of raising a child."

"I know you, Michael. You love you. What are you hiding from me? You don't need a nurse for a viral infection."

"I can hire whoever I want." Michael stood firmly planted. "I have more money and better attorneys. I really could care less what you do, but my daughter will not be raised by that crackhead. So you can either drop this whole charade or start packing Rose's things."

Gloria struggled to hold her own. "He's changed. He's been sober eight months now."

"Did he show you his gold coin?" Michael smirked. "The court does not look kindly on drug addicts."

"I'd do anything to keep my baby." She wrapped her arms around his neck, attempting to pull him closer. He tried to push her away. Instead, she slid to the floor. On her knees, she looked up him, licking her lips. "Anything, Michael."

"Have some dignity, for crissake," Michael stepped past her. "I didn't come here to have sex with you."

"Oh, I'm sorry. Who are you?" Gloria picked up one of Rose's blocks and threw it at him. "Who are you, and what did you do with Michael Dolanski?" Her face was a crumpled mess of tears and mascara. "Don't you dare threaten to take Rose from me."

He could barely breathe. "I'm not threatening you, Gloria, this is a promise."

"You don't have the balls . . ." She was on her feet.

Michael winced. "You never impressed me as the gambling type, but if this is a chance you'd like to take, go ahead. I'm just putting you on notice, keep it up, Gloria." He paused for effect. "And our next chat will be back to court."

"I wish I'd never met you. You controlling bastard. I hate you." She leapt at him, raising her hand to strike. But he caught her hand in mid-air.

"Less than two minutes ago, you were on your knees." He whispered into her ear. "While I find your groveling and lack of finesse an intriguing and somewhat amusing strategy, you can save it for some other sorry bastard. I'm not signing up for your soap opera anymore."

Emily hovered in the hallway, taking it all in. Her heart was pounding so hard that her head hurt. As Michael strode toward the door, he suddenly stopped and turned on her. "By the way, pack your things, you're fired."

Chapter 26

When the security alarm system sounded, Anni almost screamed. Since Michael had left, she heard about three things: the ocean, the housekeeper, and when she turned it on, the TV. During the day, she played tourist and visited every spot she could on Maui. In the evening, she curled up on a sofa and watched movies.

There was nothing else to do, especially since she had everything set up for Michael on Maui. In two weeks, he would begin his treatments. A couple of times, she called Joe, and they chatted for a while. She hated to admit it, but she was homesick. It was much better when Michael was there. Even in his surly moods, he was at least someone to talk to and walk on the beach with, and then the doorbell insisted. She got up and made her way to the door. It was just getting dark outside. Peeking out the peephole in the door, she couldn't believe her eyes.

"Joe! Oh, Joe!" She threw her arms around him. "I can't believe you're here. How did you get past the security system?"

"Michael gave me the code." He held her close. "Gosh, I missed you. You look wonderful." And he meant it. Rested and relaxed, this was someone he rarely saw back home. Quickly, he looked around him. "This place, oh my god, it's beautiful."

"Joe, it's heaven on earth. I'm so glad you're here." She kissed him on the cheek.

"Where's Michael and DJ?" he asked.

"They're both gone." She quickly explained. "We have this entire place to ourselves." She was breathless. "Let's go for a walk on the beach. You'll be amazed."

"Sounds perfect." He smiled. "By the way, have you ever listened to Michael's music? It's really fun."

Chapter 27

Anni had mapped out an entire week of sightseeing on the island of Maui. Their first day started with getting up in the middle of the night and heading to the eastern slopes where the famed sunrise above the clouds of Haleakala Volcano beckoned tourists to witness the splendor. She warned him to dress in layers, and they were now huddled together under a blanket in the pre-dawn chill, waiting with a growing crowd at the top of the world.

"So how did you manage to get away for two whole weeks, Joe?"

"I hadn't taken a vacation in years. I think I have a bank of about three months to use, so it wasn't a problem." He shivered. "I thought Maui would be hot all the time."

"Not in the middle of the night on a mountain. I almost froze last time." She cuddled up closer to him. "Keep me warm."

He wrapped his arm around her. "Better?"

She nodded. "I can't believe I've been here almost three weeks, and I'm still exploring."

"You came up here alone?"

She hesitated a little too long before answering. "Michael was with me."

Joe's mind did a shortcut to Michael's comment of finding a way to keep her. "Really?"

"Underneath his tough facade, he has a tender side." Anni was still smiling at her thoughts.

"Oh, I never doubted that." A tiny sliver of gold was just beginning to peek over the horizon. "It sounds like the two of you have spent a lot of time together these past few weeks?"

"We've gotten to know each other better. Actually, we have more in common than I would have ever imagined."

Joe was silent. "What about DJ?"

"He left the day after we arrived. He seems to be a busy guy, though I'm not sure what he is busy doing. He and Michael talk several times a day on the telephone. There seemed to be some urgent issue regarding replacing a nanny for his daughter. So it's just me and Michael."

Again, his mind reverted back to Michael's comment at the airport. *She's in good hands. Mine.*

"When will Michael be back?"

"Not for another three or four days. He said something about meetings with his attorney and going to visit with his daughter, Rose. Twice now, he's had me reschedule his chemo as if it's a dental appointment. I think he's in denial about his diagnosis. He doesn't want to discuss it and acts like chemotherapy is an inconvenience." She took a deep breath. "Anyway, we have a few more days to ourselves. Here comes the sunrise. You don't want to miss this."

"There are a lot of things I don't want to miss." Joe watched in awe as golden light filled the sky.

"The dawn of a new day." Anni gave him a kiss on his cheek. "I can't wait to show you more."

I can't wait to show you more. Joe thought to himself. *Is that what Michael told you?*

* * *

Surrounding herself with candles, Sera sat cross-legged on the floor of her massage studio to begin her meditation. She lined up her essential oils for healing: frankincense, lavender, and rosemary. Closing her eyes, she focused on Michael. *Oh, Great Spirit, whose voice I hear in the wind, I need your guidance and wisdom. Make my eyes and ears quick to hear your voice. Give me wisdom to understand the things you have taught my people. Help me to remain steadfast in the face of all that comes toward me. Let me learn the lessons you have hidden in the universe so that I can act with the intention of helping others. Help me find a way to help my brother, Michael. Make me always ready to do your work with a clear mind and strong hands.*

* * *

The following day, Anni had the chef prepare a picnic lunch, and they headed through Ohe'o Gulch to view the sacred pools and Waimoku Falls. It was a warm day, and Anni was wearing a halter top and shorts. With her hair pulled on top of her head and sunglasses, she looked more like a model than a nurse. He had never remembered seeing her that way in Marysville. Even her attitude seemed light as the ocean breezes.

"This place seems to suit you, Anni. I think you've found your inner Hawaiian girl."

She laughed. "It's so laid-back here, Joe. At first, I couldn't grasp it because I've always focused on being responsible and doing what others expected of me. Then Michael said, 'Go play,' and it was such a foreign concept to me. I'm embarrassed to admit it, but he finally had to show me how to have fun and relax."

"How did he do that?" It sounded more like an accusation than a question.

"Well, the first few days, he told me that I wasn't allowed to do anything. He took away my cell phone and said when I looked relaxed, he'd give it back." She laughed. "It seemed strange, but I remembered what you said about control issues, so I let it go. We just hung out by the pool, and enjoyed massages and spa treatments. He does all that stuff, manicures, facials, totally metrosexual . . ."

"What's metrosexual mean?" Joe frowned.

"Let's just say he knows how to pamper himself to look good."

"I'll bet he does."

"Oh my god, Joe." She had a way of enunciating each syllable. "Are you thinking that Michael and I are in a relationship? Are you jealous?"

He couldn't stop himself from blushing. "I've never seen you this way before. Let's face it. You're pretty and available. By any stretch of imagination, he's certainly no ordinary man. Why wouldn't you be attracted to him? Obviously, the only thing I can offer you is friendship. I can understand why you would want more out of life, why wouldn't you want someone to love, and to love you back? I have nothing to offer you, even though I want to be that person." He closed his eyes, lowering his head. "Oh god, where is the delete button when you need it?"

Anni took off her sunglasses and was quiet for a moment, then lifted his chin so she could look him squarely in the eyes. "Look at me, Joe. I mean really look at me."

She was a blur, as tears threatened to overflow and spill down his face. "No, Anni . . ."

"No. Listen to me." Her voice was soft, but firm. "One thing I've learned from being here is if you've always wanted to dance, you have to step onto the dance floor. The question you have to ask yourself is, what do you want? I want to fill my life with something I'm passionate about, something that I love so much that the day flies by. If being a priest is your passion, then give everything you have to that end. But if it's not, and there is something else that you want out there, step onto the dance floor. You might be surprised to find who will dance with you."

Chapter 28

It was the middle of the afternoon, and Michael had chosen a quiet restaurant in Malibu to conduct the interviews for a new nanny. The search had been narrowed to a woman who had almost made the cut once before. Her background checks were already completed, and her resumé included previous work for a high profile director and his wife. Since their children were getting too old for nannies, she was available. He peered over his glasses at the young woman sitting across from him.

"You have reviewed and understand the contractual agreement?"

She nodded. "Yes, sir."

"Your name is Felicia. My name is Michael. Not sir or Mr. Dolanski. Just Michael. Please call me by that name. I don't like that formal stuff." He pushed a cell phone across the table to her. "This is what you call me on. No other phones. If you have a message for me, this is a private number where I can be reached. If it's urgent, send me a text, and I'll respond."

"Got it . . . Mr . . . . ," she stammered. "Michael."

"Now, if you'll please go to page four, let's review the rules." He noticed her hands were trembling and sat back. "Felicia, I'm not trying to be mean or scary. I just need to make sure you understand. Apparently, the last nanny wasn't clear on a few key points. You are my eyes and ears. I'll be blunt. Gloria and I are not particularly fond of each other. However, Rose is my daughter and

I love her. I am depending on you to watch over her since I can't be there."

"I do understand, of course." She took a deep breath. "You also require weekly updates and a monthly report. But I must say, she's just a little girl. How much trouble can she be?"

Taking off his glasses, Michael genuinely laughed. "Rose isn't the problem. I want to know who Gloria spends time with, how she manages to mother Rose, and if she does anything that could jeopardize my relationship with my daughter. She would delight in making my life a nightmare. You just need to give me a sign, if anything seems unusual or could adversely affect me or Rose, I need to know. Your primary concern is caring for Rose. Your responsibility to me is to keep me informed. Do that, and we won't have any problems. Now do you understand?"

She took a deep breath. "You want to make sure Rose is not neglected or put in any jeopardy from people that Gloria spends her time with, and if I have any concerns about that, I'm to let you know immediately."

"That's all I'm asking of you. Are you comfortable with that arrangement?"

"Yes, sir. Michael."

Sighing, he put his glasses back on. "All right. Then let's finish here, and I'll meet you at Gloria's house in an hour. I'd like to introduce you to my daughter."

* * *

It was one of those picturesque island evenings that began with a majestic purple sunset and transcended into a silver moonlit night. Joe and Anni walked for miles on the beach, holding hands.

"Anni, I've been thinking about what you said the other day. I've come to the realization that while it's true that I became a priest for all the wrong reasons, I'm not sure I'm capable of change. This is all that I have ever known."

Anni squeezed his hand. "Have I ever told you that I never wanted to be a nurse? In my senior year in high school, I met with the guidance counselor. He asked me what I wanted to do after graduation."

"If you didn't want to be a nurse, what did you want to do?"

"I wanted to be a journalist and travel all around the world, getting the stories, reporting what I had found. Investigative reporting."

"So why didn't you?"

"The counselor told me I wasn't smart enough. I had three choices: secretary, teacher, or nurse."

"Why would anyone tell you that? You're smart, Anni. Why would you listen to him?"

"I didn't have anyone that encouraged me. I wasn't as confident or courageous as I am now. So I randomly picked nursing because being a secretary sounded boring, plus I couldn't type and being a teacher didn't seem like a good fit."

"When did you realize this was not your passion?"

"In nursing school, I used to go into the shower and cry so no one could hear me. I hated every minute of it."

"Why didn't you leave?"

"Where would I go? Joe, I had no one, no family. Back then, I thought if you start something, you had to finish it. It was like a tape playing over and over in my head. I was so insecure and lost. So I graduated and met this guy that was in my class. Tony was a nurse and kind of an adrenalin junkie. He worked in the emergency room, which was perfect for him. I liked surgery because you didn't have to interact with anyone. It's cold and impersonal. Patients come in asleep and leave asleep. I was okay with that."

"Is Tony the guy you married?"

"I married him for all the wrong reasons. I didn't love him. I'm not even sure I knew how to love anyone. I just didn't want to be alone."

"What happened to your marriage?"

"Nothing dramatic. One day we were having breakfast and I looked across the table, and asked him if he loved me."

"And he said . . ."

"No. But I already knew that. So I told him I didn't love him either, and that I was leaving. He wasn't surprised. I moved out, and after the annulment, we rarely saw each other. We didn't hate each other. Actually, I'd see him around the emergency room sometimes and we'd chat for a while. He was a nice guy. I think he married me because he felt sorry for me. It was at that point that I realized, I didn't know how to love anyone, even myself. I'd never felt that emotion before."

"We've known each other for quite a while. You've never told me that story. But Anni, that isn't the person you are today. I've never known that person."

"She doesn't exist anymore. I reinvented myself, like a rebirth. Then Michael asked me to come here, and it was like someone released me from prison. I don't know what the future holds, but I know I'm never going back there."

"Have you talked to Michael about this?"

"Michael is who told me to step onto the dance floor. I'm inviting you to do the same. I want you to come with me." She turned to him, the starlight making her look angelic. "I know how to love now, Joe. I feel that with you and have for a long time."

"It defies every logical thought in my head, but in my heart, I know you're right. I love you, too, Anni."

Under the moon, they kissed each other. Joe held her in his arms, immersed in the moment.

Joe said, "You know I've always wanted to dance with you." And she had replied, "I would love to dance."

She pulled him close, gently kissing his face. She moved from his lips and down his neck. He moaned, and she pressed her body closer to his and felt him shaking.

"I'm a priest. I've never done this before." He pulled back. "I'm sorry. I don't know what to do, Anni."

"Every dancer needs a teacher." She pulled him closer. "I'll show you."

Somehow, they managed to undress each other. Her breasts were warm, soft pillows, and he nuzzled into them. Tasting her, filling himself with her scent, he relented. And then it happened.

Oh so gently, they fell onto the beach, and she guided him. The rhythmic waves of the ocean matched the beat of his own motion as their bodies locked together. For an instant, he was lost, and had no control over what happened next. What's more, he didn't want to control anything. Suddenly, he felt a release from somewhere deep inside, and it was like he had been sick and his fever had broken. For the first time in his life, he felt strong and vibrant, ready to release himself from the past.

Anni was submerged in the moment. When he took her, she gasped at his intensity and felt more than a little overpowered by his raw emotion. Closing her eyes, she decided to ride it out and see where he took her. It was as if she had been dying of thirst, and now that she has drank from the cup, now that she had a tasted him, she wanted more. He wanted more, and she willingly complied.

Wrapping her legs around him, she pulled him even closer, if that were even possible and held onto him tightly, as if letting go, she would suddenly lose him and he would be swept out with the tide. She cried out, and he shuddered. Breathless and covered in sand, she laid her head on his chest and could hear his heart galloping against her. The pale moon cast glimmering shadows on the water, and he visualized his mother sinking to the bottom of the ocean. Enfolded in each other's arms, they submitted to each other.

The waves rolled in with the tide, the moon closed her eyes, and they fell asleep so that the sun could herald in another day. Under the diamond-studded night, Joe and Anni slept, entwined around each other like twins in the womb. Joe had one thought as he fell asleep: I like dancing.

*   *   *

At some point in the night, they made their way back to Michael's home and ended up by the pool. Anni woke up just before dawn and dove into the water, cleansing herself from their night on the beach. She hadn't skinny-dipped since her college days, but now it felt good, liberating. When Joe woke up, he watched her for a few minutes. Then he was next to her, both naked in the pool. She had to know. "About last night . . ."

"No regrets." He was gently caressing her face. "You're an amazing teacher."

Cupping his face in her hands, she kissed him deeply. "How about another dance lesson? You do seem to be a quick learner."

He laughed. "Someday I'll probably be tap dancing in hell." He pulled her ever closer. This time, they made love in the pool.

Chapter 29

Laughing, they bounded to the house, still dripping wet and wrapped in towels. She had promised to make breakfast, then they could go for a sunrise stroll on the beach. They stopped short. There was a man sitting on the sofa.

"Looks like a good morning to me." DJ was smiling broadly. "Who wants breakfast? Allow me, while you two get dressed. There are robes in a hamper next to the pool."

Anni stammered, "But we were . . ."

"Hope you like pancakes. That's my specialty. I'm not much of a morning person, so I don't do this often. You do like pancakes, right?"

Joe swallowed. "Right. Sure."

"Excellent. I can't wait to catch up with you guys. Gosh, it's good to see you both."

* * *

"I think we're in trouble," Joe was shaking. "For god's sake, we had sex in their pool. How long had DJ been there?"

"I'm sure we're not the first that ever made love in that pool." Anni wrapped the robe around her petite frame.

"Anni, we had sex." Joe said it as if he were trying to convince himself it had really happened. At the same time, he was trying to pull on his underwear. "We, you and me, we had sex, last night, this morning . . . if you recall, I'm still a priest. You think the rules weren't broken because it was in a pool? I'm just a little freaky thinking he was watching. You don't think that's creepy? Then he offers to make pancakes. Probably a prelude to kicking us out." He took a breath. "What about Michael?"

"He isn't even here." Anni took a deep breath. "We can deal with guilt later. Besides, other than DJ, no one else knows a thing."

"I hope he doesn't tell Michael."

"C'mon, let's get this awkward moment over with." Anni grabbed his hand. "Besides, I'm not going out there alone."

* * *

Joe decided it was a good time for small talk. "So, DJ, how is it you learned to fly a jet?"

"I was in the Air Force for about five years, flew missions over Afghanistan. Desert Bats, they called us." He smiled. "Pretty much means I'm a pilot."

"*Touch & Go* belongs to you?"

"Well, it's kind of on loan from my dad."

"Wow. Who gives someone a jet?" Anni joined the conversation.

"A billionaire dad." DJ was still smiling. "He owns an oil company and a couple of other commodities in Texas. I wasn't much interested in the business side. But he helped finance this venture, so I can't complain. Besides, he and Michael have diversified our portfolio and such. I'm not even sure what we own at the moment." Raising his arms, he expanded. "Oh well. What else can I say, I get to play for a living."

"So how did you and Michael meet?"

"We met in boarding school, in the band, of course. He used to come home with me, you know, weekends and summer vacations. I'm not sure but my parents may have adopted him. Sometimes I think they liked him more than me, but then I joined the Air Force and he went to college. Throughout our lives, we had both played in backyard bands, and when I came home, we discussed putting together a serious band. He was passionate about it. Truthfully,

I was lukewarm, but I'm a pilot. That's what I love, flying. Drumming is a sidebar. I just do it to hang out with Michael and the band. It took us a couple of years.

"Michael didn't want my family to pay for anything, but finally, I couldn't stand living like a pauper and went to my dad for financial support. Michael presented him with a business plan, and my father agreed to back us. In the beginning, I wasn't sure we were going to make it, then we had our first platinum hit, and we were on our way. We made enough money to pay back my father and then some. Like I said, my dad loves him." He paused.

"Michael deserves better than this. Me? I've pulled all sorts of shit. Probably used up at least eight of my allocated alley cat lives. But here I am." He poured them both some orange juice. "And now, here you are."

"Who plays keyboards?" Joe had noticed an electric keyboard in the great room.

"That would be Michael. Gina is a music teacher. Michael could probably bang piano keys before he could rollover in his crib. Personally, I think he's better on keyboards than the guitar, but don't tell him I said that. That would piss him off. He thinks he's great on both."

"I'd love to hear him play," said Joe. "I love the piano."

"Just ask him." DJ was flipping pancakes. "He loves to show off."

Anni leaned forward. "Be honest. Where does Michael disappear to at night? He just vanishes like Dracula into the night."

"That's funny that you see it that way." DJ laughed. "We have a studio here. It's totally insulated so we can jam all night and you won't hear us at all. A gift to our neighbors, I'm sure. Sometimes he works at night then sleeps most of the day. I refer to those times as his manic episodes. That doesn't happen very often, but I'll tell you, some of his best stuff comes out of those phases. Every smash hit we've ever had came from one of those bipolar nights. If I could bottle whatever that high octane shit is, we'd be unstoppable."

Anni joined in. "No wonder he wasn't too excited about our morning walks."

"He is trying to be nice to you. I've rarely seen him before noon, but then, I'm never up before noon either. If he's working, I'm usually working with him. I really do consider him to be my little brother."

Anni laughed back. "What's the story about his relationship with Rose's mother?"

"Yeah, well, talk about vampires. That would be Gloria. She tends to have a problem with honesty. Michael doesn't trust her. But he does love that little girl. He sees her as often as he can or whenever that food stamp lets him."

"What about you?" Anni pressed. "Ever married? Girlfriend?"

DJ shook his head, "Why pick a single rose when you can have the whole bouquet?" Smiling, he leaned back in his chair. "Enough about our lives, what about you guys? What's your story? I'm fascinated. I've been watching you from the beginning. I'm observant, remember?"

"There is no story." Anni was too quick.

Joe joined in. "Not really."

DJ effused. "Ah, I'm a sucker for a good romance story. I cried at that *Titanic* movie."

"You really cried?" Anni seemed impressed.

He stood up to leave, laughing. "Actually, I'm just messing with you. The only time I cried was when the old lady wasted that big-assed diamond by throwing it in the ocean. That would have been worth a couple of sweet Lamborghinis."

"I loved that movie." Anni looked as flat as her pancakes.

"Oh hey, I'm sorry, forget I said that. My bad." DJ made sad face. "Delete! I think I'm sleep-deprived. I flew half the night to get here, and in two days, I have to be back in Denver for a business meeting. I need to sleep. See you in about twelve hours. Here's my cell number, but don't call me unless it's a dire emergency. Oh, and the pool guy comes today. Just thought you'd like to know." He winked. "Good night, and if you're gonna get nasty again, lock yourself in a room."

Chapter 30

Michael actually came home a few days early. Anni immediately caught on that he was not in a good mood and left him alone. Usually, he enjoyed sitting by the pool, but now it seemed he was either behind closed doors in his studio or on the patio, off of his bedroom. From the pool, she could see him pacing, back and forth. Most of the time, pacing also coincided with him talking on his cell phone. Whatever was going on obviously had him agitated.

Though curious, she never asked him. One thing she was clear about was that she was his nurse, and even though she considered him a friend, she made every effort to keep professional boundaries with him. In all honesty, it was the most difficult job she had ever had because she really cared about him and wanted to know, as his friend. His treatments were scheduled to begin in two days. She tried to prepare him, and he basically dismissed her with a curt *"I know, Anni."* She translated that to me: *Leave me alone.* She was at a loss on how to handle him.

* * *

The day had finally arrived. Chemotherapy was scheduled to begin. Anni sat on the bed, watching Joe pack to go back to Marysville. "It won't be the same without you being here."

"It isn't the same in Marysville without you there." Joe closed the suitcase. "I haven't seen Michael yet."

"He has been sitting by the pool all night."

"I'll go check on him before I leave." Joe studied her, as she sipped on a cup of hot tea. "I wish I could stay. I don't want to go. Are you okay, Anni?"

"What's next, Joe? I'm in limbo over here."

Walking over, he sat next to her and put his arm around her. "Nothing has changed."

"Everything has changed. You said you love me. I told you that I love you. Pretty big change there, Joe." Anni kept staring at her cup. "We can't pretend this didn't happen. I feel like I've been living in a movie, and it's either time to end it or plan the sequel. What do you want?"

"I like happy endings. You know, the kind where the couple run off into the sunset and live happily ever after." He held her hand. "What about you?"

"I hate telling you this, but happily ever after doesn't fucking exist. I tried it once."

"I don't expect perfect. But I want you to hold onto this thought. I want you to be a part of my life. When I told you that I love you, I meant it." He pulled her close, kissing her tenderly. "But there are details that have to be worked out. I need some time to figure out things."

"If you're asking if I can be a mistress to a priest, that is not how I want to be part of your life. That does not work for me." Anni sat down her cup and started to walk away. "Just go talk to Michael. He needs you more than me."

"I'd never expect you to be a mistress." Joe watched her go out the door. When he heard her call after him . . .

"You do know what I want, right?" The door softly slammed behind her.

Chapter 31

He found Michael lying by the pool in the sun. "Hey, Michael."

"Hey, Joe."

"You okay?" Joe sat down in the lounge next to him.

"No, I'm far from being okay."

"You want to talk about it?"

"There's not much to say, really." Michael seemed preoccupied.

"Big stuff today. Chemotherapy."

"I don't know whether this is a beginning or an end. I guess in time, I'll have an answer."

Silence ensued.

"I'd be scared, too. Michael."

More silence.

"Actually, I'm not so much scared as I am confused by why this is happening to me. I'm not even thirty years old." Michael looked tired, and it occurred to Joe that Michael had not slept the night before.

"You've got to have hope. Without hope, you won't have the strength to fight this."

"Hope of what? I'm not sure I understand that concept. What does that mean when people say it to each other? I'm fighting for my life over here." Michael shrugged. "I hope I make it? I'm kind of thinking that cliché should be banned from our vocabulary."

Joe nodded. "Have you ever lost a fight?"

"Growing up with my mother meant I lost a few rounds."

"Now, you have a way to hit her back. Pretend cancer is your mother and chemotherapy is your weapon."

"That's a unique hypothesis, Father Darth Vader. Let's poison Mom by chemotherapy?" Michael gave him a bemused look. "Not that I would have ever connected those dots." He chuckled. "Oh, man. Part of what makes this so funny is that this philosophy is coming from a priest."

"I wasn't trying to be funny. I'm probably being obtuse."

"That's perfect, Joe. Let's redefine cancer as a bad comedy. Maybe I can live with that."

"I don't think I'm helping you." Joe blushed. "At least I'm comedic relief."

"No, actually laughing felt good." Michael sighed. "By the way, what's up with you and Ms. Anni?"

"What do you mean?" His first thought was that DJ had told Michael everything.

"Well, among other things, it looked like she just walked out on you." He hesitated. "You do know she loves you." Michael was smiling. "Can't you feel that?"

"Actually, for a while, I kind of thought the two of you . . ."

"I view her more like a sister, so you see, that would be unthinkable." Michael closed his eyes, as if in deep thought. "She is yours, if you want her. Do you want her or not?"

"I don't want anyone else to have her, if that's what you mean."

"No, it's not what I mean. You need to get out of your head and start listening to whatever you call it, God, I guess, and see where you're being led today not yesterday." Michael was in a contemplative mood.

"Maybe you were supposed to be a priest back then, but now the universe is guiding you in a different direction. In the hospital, you told me you became a priest for all the wrong reasons. So why keep reading the same book and expecting a different outcome? Would it be so bad to fall in love with Anni?"

"Did DJ tell you about the other night?"

"What should DJ be telling me?"

"Never mind. Yes, I love her, okay?"

"My question still stands: You have a dilemma. How are you going to handle it?"

"Actually, I came out here to talk to you about your chemotherapy."

"You're not listening to me. What are you going to do about it? Anni deserves an answer."

Joe felt blindsided. "I don't know what to do, Michael."

"Remember when I told you I have a spiritual side? Here it is. First of all, I definitely don't believe in coincidence or random acts. I believe that everything is interconnected. Every person, animal, and plant has a spirit. Even earth itself has a spirit or essence. People come into our lives because of these interconnections. For the record, I think you and Anni have a connection or destiny together. For example, I was lead to DJ and his family. They helped me find my way in the world and believed in me. Without them, I wouldn't be here today."

"Do you mean that God guides us to those people and places?"

"God is what you choose to call your belief in something greater than yourself. I choose to think of it as a universal truth or wisdom. I think there are spiritual interventions that happen all around us, but sometimes we are tuned out and don't hear the messages. We think it is a coincidence. Do you think you and Anni were just randomly thrown together and came here to help me?"

"I'm not clear. What is our role in all this? Just to wait and see what happens next?"

"Well, no offense, but that's what you do. Aside from spiritualism, while we are here on earth, we are supposed to learn lessons from each other. Sometimes it takes us a few jogs around the block before we learn the lesson, so the lesson will keep reappearing in some form until we stick the landing, as DJ would say."

"Do you believe in angels?"

"Well, let me try to explain this," Michael sighed. "I believe there are spirit guides and guardian angels. Spirit guides are humans and here with us on earth. They are old souls with great wisdom and are here to assist us in many ways. Shamans and healers are spirit guides. Guardian angels have been sent or chosen to watch over you on this earthly plane. Their role is much different from spirit guides."

Joe nodded. "I believe in saints and angels and can embrace divine intervention. We're on the same note there." Joe paused. "Where did you learn this philosophy?"

"Her name is Seraphine, and she was my best friend in high school." Michael opened his eyes. "Oh my god, I get it." He broke into a wide smile. "This is perfect. Thank you for this conversation, Joe."

"How did I help you? I was the one being obtuse."

Michael laughed. "I need to listen to my own advice. Turn up the volume of those spirit guides!" He gave Joe a hug. "Thanks. Good talk. I know what I need to do now."

* * *

First, Michael went to his bedroom. He had already searched in all the obvious places: the nightstand next to his bed, his suitcases, even the pocket of his robe. "I'm sure I wouldn't have thrown that out." Now, he sat at his desk in the studio.

"Where did I put that piece of paper?" It wasn't in his desk drawer or in one of his neat stacks. In desperation, he picked up his cell phone and dialed information. "Marysville, California. Seraphine Rosewood." He waited. "No one has landlines anymore."

The nameless voice responded. "I'm sorry, we don't have a listing for anyone by that name."

"Okay, thanks." He dialed again. "Gina, it's Michael."

"Hi honey, are you all right?" Gina sounded concerned. "Did you have your chemo yet?"

"I'll be going over there in a few minutes. I have a favor to ask you."

"What can I do?"

"I'm trying to locate Sera. I think she said she works at the hospital, but I'm not sure. She gave me her number, but I think I lost it. I need to talk to her."

There was a silent pause on the other end of the line. "May I ask why this is so urgent?"

"Gina," Michael snapped. "Just find her number and send me a text message, okay?"

Someone knocked on the door. Anni stepped inside. "We have to go now."

"Please, Gina, it's important to me."

Chapter 32

The hospital had provided Michael with a private room. There were forms to sign and side effects to go over: flulike symptoms, low white counts, extreme exhaustion, taste changes, ringing in the ears, hair loss, pins and needles in fingers and toes, nausea, mouth sores, low red counts, easy bruising, metallic taste in the mouth, the list never seemed to end. Then there was something about a port line that they needed to place in his chest, so they could administer the medications, a cocktail of poison that was supposed to be a cure. To Michael, the cure alone could kill you.

For a minute, he sat immobilized on the edge of the hospital bed, trying to focus. Anni could see his hands were shaking. Without any warning, he threw all the papers to the floor as if they had spontaneously combusted.

"I've changed my mind. I can't go through with this. I honestly think I'd rather die." His breathing was rapid and shallow. "Where's Joe? Why isn't he here with me?"

Anni was at his side. "Michael. Listen to me." She grabbed his arm. "Michael!"

But he couldn't hear her. Placing his hands over his throat, he acted like he couldn't catch his breath. Anni punched the call light to get someone in there who could help.

DJ sauntered into the room and stopped. "What the hell is going on in here?"

"He's having a panic attack." Anni turned to DJ. "Stay with him. I have to call Joe."

* * *

"Flight 1205, now boarding for Los Angeles." From LA, he would catch a plane to Sacramento.

Joe had turned the ringer off on his phone, placing it on vibrate. His bags were checked, except the one he was carrying on. Stepping into the line, he began to proceed to the gate. At first, he decided to ignore the buzzing. It stopped. Good. He showed the woman his boarding pass. She nodded. Passing the gate, he was on his way and just about to the door to enter the plane. It vibrated again. Frowning, he pulled the phone out of his pocket. What could possibly be so important? He saw it was Anni and immediately stepped aside. People were pushing past him, trying to board the plane.

"Anni?"

"Get over here now."

"What's wrong?"

"He panicked and is refusing treatment. He wants you."

"I'm on my way."

By the time Joe arrived, Michael had been given a sedative and had calmed down some, but that didn't mean he was any bit closer to being agreeable to chemotherapy.

"This isn't medicine, it's poison. I don't want this, I want to go home, Joe."

"I understand. But you have to go through with this. Michael, you don't have any other options. If you don't, you will die. All these side effects are temporary. There are medications to help you tolerate the side effects." He turned, "Isn't that right, Anni?"

Anni nodded. "I promise. I'll stay right beside you. Whatever you need, I'm here."

Michael was squeezing Joe's hand so tight that it was painful. "Will you both stay? I've never been so scared in my whole life."

Anni and Joe looked at each other. Joe nodded. "We'll both stay. But you have to let them put in the port. The sooner we start, the sooner we can all go back home."

"Please don't leave me alone."

"We'll both stay until you kick us out." Joe was losing feeling in his hand. "Deal?"

Michael nodded.

They circled his bed. DJ was there, holding one hand, while Joe held the other hand. Anni gently stroked his forehead. His breathing slowed. Color returned to his face. Crisis averted, for now. The port line was inserted. Michael dozed. About an hour later, a nurse and the doctor brought in the elixir and started his first chemotherapy treatment. Michael opened his eyes and for a moment, and it looked like the whole scene was going to play out again.

"I feel like I'm on death row." His breathing quickened, eyes wide.

Anni took over. "It's okay. Close your eyes. In a little while, it will be all over, and we can go home."

Actually, he was going to have to stay for another couple days to get in his radiation treatment before he went home. But no one dared to tell him that right now.

In the meantime, DJ looked to Joe and Anni. The treatment was over, and Michael was sleeping. "What in hell went down here today?"

Anni started. "He panicked and changed his mind. I'm sorry. I thought he was prepared."

DJ pointed to the door. "All right. We need an emergency foxhole meeting. Now."

They slumped behind, following him into the hallway, staring at the floor. Anni whispered to Joe, "I feel like I've just been summoned to the principal's office."

DJ faced them both. "Obviously, Michael wants both of you here. Joe, if you can stay, I'll make certain you are compensated. If not, I'll figure out a way to make Michael understand. But we can't have this scenario every time he goes for a treatment."

"Well, you know I'm here for the duration." said Anni. "I'm staying."

"I know that. You are already employed as a private duty nurse for Dolanski & Jansen Incorporated." He turned to Joe. "What about you? Can you stay? I think Anni is going to need back up."

"I really don't know what I can offer, other than support."

"As a priest, what's that like, I mean financially. I don't have a clue."

"Well, they factor housing and expenses into my salary."

DJ snorted. "Just give me a number I can work with."

"I don't know. Maybe $40,000 a year."

DJ shook his head. "All right, look, I don't have a choice. I don't have the luxury of staying with him throughout this ordeal, so I need you guys. I am covering everything for Michael so he can take this time to recover. I'm on double duty right now. That's why I'm gone so much of the time. I hate treating friends like staff, but I have to do this legitimately. Anni, I can justify your role. Joe, can you be her assistant or something?"

"Well, I will have to contact the Bishop and request a leave of absence. They would need to find another priest. I may need some time . . ."

"I don't understand. Michael wants you here. I need to know right now because I have to fly to Dallas in the morning to meet with my father. He wants to know what's going on with Michael, and I'd rather tell him in person. As I said before, Michael is like a son to him."

Anni was staring at Joe, her eyes searching for his answer.

"Let me call the bishop. But I'll stay. I want to help." He heard Anni let out a soul-deep sigh.

DJ sighed too. "Joe, I'll get a contract together for you while I'm in Dallas. Anni, I'm sure you already completed some of these forms before you came here. But let me make sure everything is in order. You both have new jobs and now live on Maui."

Chapter 33

They had been home for a week. The second day, Michael had spiked a fever, and they had to call the oncologist. The concern was that he was having an adverse reaction to one of the drugs. Anni monitored him closely. Twenty-four hours later, he improved. He had some nausea, but otherwise he had tolerated the first round without major complications.

Joe and Anni were standing in the kitchen. He pulled Anni next to him. "I have to go back to Marysville at some point. I need to meet with the bishop."

"I put my house on the market. My neighbor is going to keep my cat. I'm not going back. They have already posted my position at the hospital. Not that I'll miss that place."

"Does this feel surreal, or is it just me?"

Anni nodded. "I know. Overnight, our entire lives have changed. I feel like we won the lottery or something."

Joe took a deep breath. "Except we're here because Michael is sick."

"Sometimes I feel guilty because I'm so happy here."

"Hey, you feel up to a late night swim?"

Anni pulled him close, kissing him soundly. "I'm up for another dance if you are."

Joe took the freedom of letting his hands roam. He could smell her, taste her, and his senses were suddenly aroused. She pressed closer and then . . . Michael sauntered into the kitchen, his expression deadpan.

Anni and Joe both jumped back at the same time. Anni spoke, "We didn't realize you were awake."

"Obviously." Michael opened the refrigerator door and closed it without even looking. "Please don't stop on my account. I enjoy signs of life."

"We were just about to make . . . ," Anni started.

Michael put up his hand. "I don't need details."

". . . something to eat," she finished.

He half-smiled. "Joe does seem hungry." Plopping into the nearest chair, he sighed. "Rewind to the going back to Marysville part. Did I hear that correctly?"

They both sat down. Joe took the lead. "We both have a lot of loose ends. Real estate, storage, selling stuff, not to mention, I have to meet with the bishop."

"Enlighten me. This bishop. Something like the local pope?"

Anni stifled a laugh. "That's kind of like Joe's boss."

"I thought you priests had a direct hotline to God? Oh well. That kind of narrows our options to door number two and three." He hesitated. "Anni, did you make coffee?"

"Yeah. I'll get some. Joe?"

"Sure, I'll have some coffee, too." Joe cleared his throat. "Okay, here's the thing. I could ask for a transfer, but I doubt there are many openings for a priest in Maui. If there were, we'd all be scrambling to live here. Secondly, I can't just walk away like being a priest didn't matter. I have responsibilities, obligations. Though, at this point, he might remove me from my position for abandonment of duties."

Anni stepped in. "It's not that easy to leave your entire life behind."

Michael leaned back in his chair, shaking his head. "What is it with your generation? Have some vision. Don't you see? What difference does it make if the bishop fires you? Do you really want that man in charge of your destiny? Tell me why that's a good life plan, because you're right, I don't get it.

"Joe, you can make more money managing one of my juice bars, and Anni, you do realize you are not going to be my nurse forever. I'm either going to get well or die. That's pretty much my door number one and two. At that point, you will both need another plan. I say we start working on that now.

"But know this, no matter what happens to me, I will make certain your futures are secure. You have been loyal to me, and I will pay that back. I wouldn't be so narcissistic as to ask you to give up your lives and come here, then not watch out for you. Just tell me what would you like to do?"

They were both silent. Joe finally broke the silence. "Anni and I need to talk."

"Sure, of course, I just threw a lot at you." Michael stood up. "You know, I think breakfast does sound good. Why don't I take the lead on that? I think I saw some yogurt and fresh fruit in the refrigerator." He winked at them. "You see, I have culinary skills, too."

Chapter 34

"**I'm going back** to Marysville in the morning, Anni."

Joe and Anni were walking on the beach. The wind was swirling black clouds into the blue spaces, the way a child might paint outside the lines.

Anni managed to nod. "At some point, I knew you would."

"I'll be back in a few weeks, in plenty of time for Michael's next chemo treatment. I have to meet with the bishop."

Anni did that little snort. "Did you tell Michael?"

"We talked."

The wind was blowing her hair across her face, obscuring her expression. "Okay. But I'm staying. I have nothing to go back for now."

"You're not listening." He put his arm around her, turning her toward him. "I said I'll be back in a few weeks."

"So what is this meeting about with the bishop?"

"I want to talk with him. I want to explain everything to him in person. I owe him that respect."

Chapter 35

"**We have to at least** make an appearance." Michael was reviewing their upcoming schedule.

"Are you up for this?" DJ said. "Can you even sing? I mean radiation to the lungs..."

Michael didn't look convinced. "At least I can try. Anni is pissed at me. She doesn't want me to go. She doesn't understand why this is important."

"How much time do we have?"

"A couple weeks, I think, not much more until my next chemo treatment."

"What if you get sick?"

"If all I have to do is show up and look pretty, DJ. I can do that." They were sitting in their studio. Everything on the desk had been tidily arranged in neat Michael stacks: upcoming schedules, financial ledgers, and new business proposals.

DJ nodded. "Hurling on stage wouldn't look pretty. This is the biggest music award show in Hollywood. We're up for song of the year. We have been asked to perform that song live. That's a huge honor, Michael."

"I know what it means." Michael looked at everything on the desk and sat back. "My suggestion would be that we need to get everyone together and start rehearsing. But I'm not sure I can sing after all this radiation to my lungs. Can we secure the studio in Honolulu?"

DJ nodded again. "I've already reserved it." He hesitated. "What about lip syncing? I know you wouldn't want to do that, but it would be better than watching you collapse on stage."

"That's a good idea, DJ." Michael took a deep breath. "As long as I'm fairly stationary, no dancing and moving around, I think I can manage. We could arrange for dancers on stage, so there is action, but it wouldn't require me to perform." He sighed. "The biggest night of our lives, and I have to be sick. After the ceremony, I need you to hit the parties for me. It's taking all I have just to make this trip. Afterward, I'm going to Marysville with Gina for a few days."

"I'm sorry. Did I just hear you say you're going to Marysville? Whatever for?"

"I know. But I'm trying to find someone. I asked Gina to help me, and she's worthless." Michael took off his glasses and threw them onto the desk. "She never liked her. I think Gina is purposefully ignoring me. So I'm going to find her on my own."

"Well, I don't know who is so important, but this sounds like a quest. All I can say is she must have been really good."

"It's not like that. She knows my heart and soul. We belong together."

"Okay, sure. Call it whatever you want." He paused. "Do you mind if I use that line in the future?"

"Put a zipper on it, DJ." Michael snapped. "I need her."

"Maybe we all need her." He saw Michael glaring at him and tried not to laugh. "Okay, okay, I'm sorry. This is not sexual. Got it."

Michael looked like he wanted to slap him. "Nothing sexual is going on over here, and thanks for noticing. The only thing I've been hugging is a porcelain toilet. Please, shut the fuck up."

"Okay. Time for a subject change." DJ backed away. "But I do have one question before we totally close the chapter on this topic. God forbid I tell you what to do, but since Joe is in Marysville, maybe he can help you find this guru or whatever she is." DJ tried to redeem himself. "Actually, I'm kinda surprised you didn't think of that yourself."

"Dear lord, why didn't I think of that?" He smacked himself on the forehead. "Of course. She works in the hospital. Joe is at the hospital. What is the matter with me?" Michael ran his fingers through his hair. A large clump fell to the floor. "Oh. My. God." Neither of them moved, staring at the clump as if a tarantula had parked itself there.

"Better get a wig." DJ mumbled. "Either that or a new look."

When neither of them made a move to pick it up, DJ put his arm around Michael and led him out of the office, locking the door behind them.

Chapter 36

It was late afternoon, and Joe was in the refectory office, still in the process of clearing his desk, his calendar and his life. Piles had turned into a horder-sized mountain of mail, bills, and messages. In about an hour, he had to perform mass, then it would be time to go back to his apartment to continue the purge. Someone knocked on his door. Not a good time for interruptions. He ignored it. Insistently, whoever it was knocked again.

Sighing, he got up and opened the door. "Yes?" It was a woman, clearly of Native American descent. She had waist-length jet black hair and exquisite high cheekbones. There was something about her that was both exotic and strikingly beautiful. He didn't recognize her. "Can I help you?"

"I think I can help you."

* * *

It was a quiet night on the island. Hidden safely on the darkened lanai, Anni couldn't see the waves, but she could hear them, rolling in, rolling out, rolling in with perfect timing. The night was warm, but comfortable. Soft breezes and just a hint of jasmine in the air beckoned the stars to come out in a brilliance she had never seen before, as if God had flung diamonds into the night sky, just for her pleasure.

Closing her eyes, she leaned back and breathed in peace. After a while, she slid into a trance, rolling in and rolling out with the ocean, the night breeze cleansing away any disharmony. Her breathing slowed, in and out. Her limbs felt heavy, weighed down by the waves, and then light again as she was swept out to sea, the waves now carrying her, supporting her body as she floated on starlit waves. Glistening beneath her, drifting in and out of consciousness . . .

Somewhere, a clock chimed nine times. That is when she remembered. "The awards show." Hurriedly, she headed for what was referred to as the theater. DJ had once shown her how to turn everything on. It was time to find out if she had been a good student. After a few unsuccessful tries, she found the manual. Step one, now step two, rock 'n' roll. Suddenly, the room was filled with music and the lights automatically dimmed. "Sweet. All I need is some popcorn." She got cozy, ready to watch the show, adding, "And a friend would be nice."

* * *

"I'm sorry." Joe ushered her into his office. "Are you a parishioner here?"

"No. I'm a friend of someone you know. Quite well, I guess."

"Oh." He sat down behind his desk. Gesturing toward the piles, he said, "I've been out of town. Sorry about all this. I didn't catch your name. We have a mutual friend?"

"Michael Dolanski."

"Ah . . ." He was amazed at the length fans would go to meet a star.

She read his mind. "It's not like that. I'm not a fan. Actually, I visited him in the hospital."

"Excuse me, I'm confused. Who are you?"

"Seraphine Rosewood. Michael and I were friends in high school."

"Seraphine . . ." He leaned back. It sounded familiar. He'd heard that name before. "You said something about helping me? No offense, but why do I need help?"

"I heard you and the nurse talking in the restroom. I know he has cancer. His sister will only ignore me. But you, you have a connection with him. I spoke with him before he left the hospital. We have history. Ask him." She stood before him, her eyes begging. "Please. There's no hidden agenda. Here's my number. Tell him to call me. If you let me, I can help you with him. I know how to help him."

Joe's cell phone was lying on the desk, vibrating. He looked down, and to his amazement saw it was Michael. He looked up at the woman sitting across from him. Her eyes fell to the phone. When Joe didn't answer it, Michael left a text message:

I'm trying to find Seraphine Rosewood. Can u help me???

Joe picked up the phone, handing it to Sera. "It's for you."

Chapter 37

Sera took the phone and texted him back.
*** *OMG. It's Sera. R U psychic? I am sitting in Joe's office! Trying to find you.*
*** *I need your address. I have a surprise for you*
*** *Can you call me?*
*** *No privacy. Gina glue . . .* ☺
*** *OK. Here you go . . .*
After, she finished sending her address, she handed the phone back to Joe. "Thank you."

Joe shook his head. "I don't think I've ever seen anything like that happen. What a coincidence."

She smiled at him. "I don't believe in coincidences, do you?"

He smiled back. "Not anymore."

* * *

Backstage after the award ceremony, everyone was bathing in the afterglow of success. Michael was posing with their trophy, sporting a new look and everyone said he looked great with a shorter, punkier hairstyle. Next on the agenda for most stars: party central all night long. Instead, Michael was going back to Marysville with Gina in the morning. DJ offered to circulate, willing to play party boy for the night.

The evening had more than one high point. Michael also ran into Nick Paradise. Cameras rolling . . .

"Hey Michael, I don't want any shit with you."

"Then stay away from my baby girl." The crowds pressed around them, the hum of chatter and loud music obliterated their words.

"Actually, Gloria postponed our wedding. She said she needed more time, that she wasn't ready for a commitment. I think you had something to do with that, you fucking prima donna bully."

Michael smiled, waving at the cameras. "I'll see to it you are committed for a long time if you set one foot near my Rose. You walking meth lab."

Both men parted ways, shaking hands with fans and the press, congratulating each other on their successes. Later, the news media reported that good sportsmanship had won the day.

* * *

Chapter 38

Joe had never been in the bishop's office. It was more like a library with bookshelves to the ceiling. His desk was as large as a ping-pong table. He looked at his watch. He had been waiting for almost thirty minutes. Finally, the bishop made his grand entrance, though actually he looked more he had just returned from the gym.

"Sorry to keep you waiting. I got stuck in traffic. You know how that is." He smiled at him.

"Actually, I've never seen a traffic jam in Marysville." Joe tried to focus on just breathing. "It's pretty quiet there, most of the time, except of course, for the prune festival."

"Ah yes, I've never attended. So what's it like in Maui? I imagine there are lots of tourists?" Finally, he sat down behind his desk. "I've always wanted to go there. Maybe I will someday."

"You definitely should. It's beautiful beyond words."

"Yes, I'll add that to my list of places to visit." The bishop sat back. "But I'm surmising you didn't come to me to talk about my vacation plans."

"I wish it were that easy." He almost felt dizzy from the lack of oxygen.

"I'm concerned about your lack of presence in the parish over the past few months. Can you explain the importance of this leave of absence? My understanding is that you have been caring for a rock star that is ill?"

"That's correct, but technically he's not a rock star."

"All right, musician. You're a good priest, Joe. I don't want to lose you. Let me help you."

Joe had never imagined this day. What he had to say next seemed implausible to the point that he felt like someone else was speaking. "I have fallen in love with a woman. We've been friends for the past few years, but I realize now that has changed, and I want to be with her. While I will always love the church, and it's been an honor to serve, I know it's time for me to go."

The bishop walked over and sat down next to him, putting his arm around Joe's shoulder. "You're not the first priest that has ever fallen in love. Are you sure about this decision?"

"For the first time in my life, I have never been as sure about anything."

The bishop nodded. "I know you wouldn't come to this decision lightly. I appreciate your trust in me. While I am sad to lose you, I want you to be happy. Go in peace, Joe. I will initiate the necessary paperwork to release you from the priesthood, though it may take a while before everything is completed."

Joe managed to whisper. "Thank you."

* * *

It had been a long, exhausting day at the spa which had included eight full body massages and two detoxification body treatments with seaweed wraps. Sera was putting away clean sheets for tomorrow's appointments and disinfecting her massage table, then she was going home to zone out with a movie.

She heard the chime at the door of her studio. Frowning, she knew there were no clients coming this late in the evening. At first, she decided to ignore it, but when it chimed again, she decided to go see who was there. Peeking through the tiny hole in the door, she saw . . . "Michael?"

He smiled at her. "I don't suppose you still have that old pickup truck? I'd like to go back to the Indian burial grounds."

* * *

Once again, they sat cross-legged on top of the burial grounds of her elders, holding hands.

She squeezed his hands. "Close your eyes, Michael. Tell me what you hear."

He obeyed her command. "I hear my heart beating."

"What do you feel?" she asked.

"I feel at home with you." He smiled.

She smiled back. "What do you see?"

He opened his eyes. "I see you, Sera." He leaned over, pulling her close, kissing her face, lost in her long, dark hair. "I realized that in my life, there was no one that accepted me like you. And I . . . I have never felt this way with anyone else. Over the years, I thought about you, but I was too embarrassed to contact you. I can't explain it, but it's like you are a part of me. When I'm with you, I am free to be myself. I don't have to pretend. I feel safe with you. Please come home with me, Seraphine. I know now we're supposed to be together. I've always loved you."

Sera nodded, her eyes brimming with tears. "Welcome home, Michael."

Chapter 39

Anni was a giant ball of stress. Michael was supposed to be at Maui Medical Center tomorrow for chemo, and she hadn't heard a peep out of him. She sent him a text message.

*** *where r u? Chemo scheduled for 2 morrow??*

Michael replied: *will be there. Sera will b there with me. U R off the hook.* ☺

*** *No, I'm your nurse??*

*** *I'm OK. C U at home after chemo.*

She sighed to herself. *Now what?* Joe had told her that Michael would probably be bringing home a girlfriend. But it was her responsibility to oversee his care. She debated on whether to meet him there anyway. This was his third out of four treatments. She opted to let it go, but made a promise to discuss this issue with Michael when he returned.

* * *

It had been more than a week since the awards ceremony. "How's Michael?" Joe had called Anni for an update.

"This was his next to last round for chemo. His white cells are low, so he's extremely fatigued. Plus, he doesn't eat or drink much of anything because he said he everything tastes awful. I'm worried he is going to get dehydrated."

"What did the oncologist say?"

"She said this is typical."

"What does that mean?"

"The side effects are expected, but hopefully he should improve in a few weeks."

Joe paused. "Hopefully? How are you? Are you okay?"

"I'm doing all right, I think..."

"Where's DJ?"

"He's anywhere but here." Anni sounded resigned.

"You're alone?"

"No, actually there is a woman here that Michael is very attached to, I think you know her. Seraphine. She rarely leaves his side, and if she does, he finds her."

Smiling to himself, he said, "I know. I met her in Marysville. I'll have to tell you that story. But I wanted to tell you in person. Michael's going to be fine now."

"It's almost hard to do my job. She wants to do everything for him and that seems to be what he wants, too. She went for his chemo treatment, and I was left out. For god's sake, I'm his nurse. I'm supposed to be there."

"Have you had a chance to visit with her yet?"

"Not unless you consider 'pass the puke bucket' a meaningful dialogue."

Joe chuckled. "Well, I think we're going to get to know her very soon. If you ask me, she has definitely joined our little family."

Chapter 40

"**I'm so sorry**, Anni. I just want to shower and wash my hair, I feel so disgusting . . ." Michael was struggling to get out of his bed.

Anni heard a voice behind her. DJ had apparently returned.

"I'm here, Michael. C'mon, buddy, let's go." DJ lifted him off the bed like a small child.

"I hate this." Michael balked.

"It won't last. You'll be better soon. Right, Anni?"

Anni wanted to cry, partly from exhaustion, partly from relief. "Thanks, DJ."

Once DJ got Michael situated, he motioned for Anni to follow him down the hall. As they left the room, Sera simply walked past them and, with slight nod of acknowledgement, went in and sat down on Michael's bed.

"When is Joe coming back?"

"I just got off the phone with him. I'll call him."

DJ was in a mood. "I'm counting on you guys. Michael's job is to recover. I have to work. Your job is to take care of everything so I can do that. Joe's job is to cover you. Pretty simple plan as I see it."

"Understood." She prayed Joe would understand.

"By the way, who's the Indian chick?" DJ was frowning.

"Michael went to Marysville, and she came home with him. They're inseparable."

"Oh yeah, that's right." DJ shook his head. "His childhood friend or something?"

Anni nodded. "They do meditations daily. Michael is a different person with her."

"If it makes him feel better, I'm cool with that." DJ shrugged. "But I'm going to stick around for a while. No one is going to take advantage of him. I'll personally see to that."

* * *

Since Michael was sleeping, Sera decided to explore her new surroundings. Pushing open the door, she lightly trotted to the beach. It was dawn, and unusually peaceful and isolated, which was exactly what she needed. Surrounded by nothing but a few joggers, she kicked off her shoes and began to run. Cool gritty sand shifted and melted under her feet. Foamy grey water swirled around her ankles. Running harder, tears swelled up, overflowing down her cheeks.

After a few miles, she fell to the beach, closing her eyes. *Thank you for this gift. Keep me still so I can hear your voice in the wind and know the direction to take, so that I can help Michael.* Her heartbeat began to slow, and she filled her lungs with the salt-fine spray melting into the sand. She wasn't sure how long she lay there, thinking, but her first two days in Maui had been a hard landing.

First, there was the chemo treatment and Michael's violent reaction. She had never seen anyone go through chemo, but it was more than a little intimidating. While she wasn't sure what to do, she knew Michael wanted her there, and she wanted to be supportive. But it felt like every time she tried to help, she only got in Anni's way. Of course, they were both superficially polite, but it seemed that Anni kept a watchful eye on her. Though that made sense, because, in fact, Anni didn't know anything at all about her.

She took one last deep breath and rose to her feet. Michael would be awake soon. She spoke to the wind. *"I'm releasing any negativity, so that my guides can show me the way. My heart and intentions are pure. Let them see that, and know I mean no harm."* It was time to go back.

*   *   *

Fortunately, DJ kept his promise. Anni handled days, but at night, Sera stayed with him. Mostly, Michael slept between bouts of sleeping and getting sick. It became a kind of routine, sleep, puke, sleep. Anni had felt like she was sleepwalking. Now at least, Sera was another helper. There was one day that was particularly bad, and since Sera had been up all night, she was napping in one of the guest rooms. Worn out, Anni and DJ literally fell asleep next to each other at the foot of Michael's bed.

"Anni?"

"DJ."

"Michael's sick again." DJ yawned.

"I know."

"You're up." DJ pushed her.

"No. It's your turn." She pushed back.

"I think it's your turn."

"Okay." Anni dozed off again.

By sunset, Anni found herself nuzzled into DJ's lap, his arm protectively around her. Slowly, she sat up, trying not to wake him as she extracted herself from his limp embrace. Peering toward the bed, she realized Michael was gone. Frowning, she tiptoed to the bathroom. He wasn't there. Silently, she closed the door behind her, not wanting to wake DJ. He was sound asleep.

Michael was sitting in the kitchen, sipping on a mug of steaming hot tea.

"What are you doing?" Anni blinked.

"I think I'm dehydrated. But I feel somewhat better, so I made myself some ginger tea. Sera said it's supposed to help if you feel sick. I think it's working. You want some? You don't look so hot."

"Yeah. Sounds good."

Michael got her a mug and poured some for her. "Oh, you and DJ. Were you aware you had your face buried in his crotch?"

Anni blushed. "Six months ago, if someone had told me that, I would have thought they were on drugs."

He laughed softly. "Thanks for being on puke detail. Please tell me things will get better from this point on." He poured himself more tea. "I want my life back. I'm tired of this being sick stuff. When can we expect to see Joe again?"

"Soon, I think. I haven't had a chance to tell you, but congratulations on song of the year."

"You watched the award ceremony?"

"Are you kidding? I thought it was sweet to see your sister there. Gina looked like she was going to burst with pride when you put your arm around her and thanked her for teaching you how play the guitar and the keyboards. I can tell you really love each other."

Michael actually blushed. "Secretly, she's my mom."

Anni smiled, "So I haven't had much time to talk with you, but tell me about Seraphine. Of course, we met briefly, but I haven't had a chance to get to know her yet."

"I'm sorry about that. When we arrived, we went straight to the hospital for my treatment. Not a very good way to introduce all of you. For that, I apologize."

"How did the treatment go?" Usually, she was there, holding his hand. "You know as your nurse I'm obliged to be there, right?"

He nodded. "Sera stayed with me. I was okay, Anni. Mostly, I slept."

"That's sure different from your first time around."

"Yeah," Michael sighed. "I'm learning it's better for everyone if I just stay calm and accept there are some things I can't change."

"That's huge, Michael," Anni was impressed. "How did this transformation take place?"

"Well, you're going to have to meet Sera." Michael's face was total peace. "When I'm with her, I feel like everything that was wrong is suddenly going to be all right. I don't know how to explain it. She makes me want to be a better person. I respect her and trust her." He laughed. "I sound like an idiot, don't I?"

"No." Anni put down her cup and hugged him. "You sound like someone in love."

Chapter 41

Later that day, Anni accidentally got her chance to meet Sera. Anni was walking alone on the beach, when she looked up and saw Sera walking toward her. Both women stopped and looked at each other. Sera smiled shyly at her.

Since Anni was older, she figured it was her job to be the mature one and go first. "Since we now live together, I think it's time to at least say hello. I'm Anni Cavatini."

"Seraphine Rosewood. I remember seeing you at the hospital."

Anni nodded. "You want to walk with me?"

"I'd like that. I love walking on the beach. I never imagined living in a place where you could just walk out your door and there you are. Actually, it feels like I dropped in on another planet. It's so different from Marysville."

"I felt the same way at first." Anni smiled back. "But you'll get used to it really quick. And Michael's home, well, it's actually a mansion. I think we all live by the pool."

"I haven't had a chance to see much of anything, but so far, it's impressive." She shrugged. "I did not grow up like that."

"Neither did Michael." Anni really looked at her. Sera was rather tall and willowy. She was exquisite, with fine features and long black hair. In a way, she and Michael were a lot alike, which made her wonder if Michael had some Native American ancestry. "Do you mind my asking how you and Michael met? I've never heard the story. The only thing I've heard is that you were childhood sweethearts."

Sera laughed. "Well, not exactly. I think we were fifteen years old, so we were teenagers. But I certainly remember the first time I met him . . ." She told Anni the whole story, never sparing any details. "I thought Gina sent him away so we couldn't be together. I was so angry with her."

"So what happened to you after Michael left?"

"I know this probably doesn't make any sense, but I couldn't even consider dating anyone. I felt like I had lost an arm or something. Part of me was missing. When Thanksgiving or Christmas came, I thought he would surely be at home. But he never came back to Marysville. I'd make popcorn and fudge, our favorite together, and just sit and cry. I missed him so much."

"This was more than a crush. You really loved him?"

Sera nodded. "I tried dating, but it never worked out. No one compared to Michael. Finally, I went to school and became a massage therapist. I settled into a life of work and routine responsibility. By day, I worked, and at night I went home. I decided this was my life. When Michael came back to Marysville, I was obsessed with seeing him again. He was the first and only person I ever truly loved."

Anni was quietly thinking. "Michael has mentioned that his mother had mental problems and could be abusive, but he never shared details with me."

"I witnessed her being abusive to Michael. She was cruel to him, and it broke my heart. My own family was dysfunctional, but this was beyond that." She flashed back to the night on the porch. "My mother died a few years ago, and I'm not close to my brothers and sisters. I felt alone in the world. When I was with Michael, I felt connected to something, and I can't explain it. I just know that without him, I felt lost."

Anni pressed on. "So did you grow up in Marysville? I know you are Native American."

"I never lived on a reservation, though my grandparents did. When I was little, we moved around a lot, but we finally settled in California. My father worked a variety of jobs, but mostly, he was a farmer, I guess. I know he worked in the vineyards. I came from a large family. Lots of brothers and sisters. You'd think that made us close to each other, but we weren't. My father had a drinking problem, so he lost jobs, and then we'd move again to someplace where he could find work. What about you, Anni?"

Anni gave her a quick synopsis of growing up in foster homes and how she ended up in Marysville, ending with how she met Michael, moved to Maui and her life changed.

"I'm a little confused about something."

"What's that?" Sera frowned.

"Usually, when a child is neglected or abused, protective services gets involved. Nurses, social workers, and the police would be required to file a report and that child would be removed from the home and could be placed in foster care."

"I'm not following you." Sera stopped. "What are you saying?"

"Oh, nothing. I was just wondering why no one helped Michael. It's kind of amazing to me that he managed to escape that environment and not have emotional problems. At the very least, I think I'd have post-traumatic syndrome or something."

Sera nodded. "He is a strong person. It is one of the things I admire about him."

"Hmmm . . ." Anni changed the subject. "When you left Marysville to come to Maui, what did you do with your home and business?"

"The house was rented, so I just put everything in storage. As for my business, I just closed it."

"Well, I'm glad you're here. Michael is obviously very much in love with you." Anni smiled. "I'm going to jog back. I'll see you back at the Dolanski estate?"

"Thanks for inviting me to tag along." Sera smiled back.

After Sera left, Anni started jogging back home, but thought to herself: *Gina wasn't wealthy and even if she held down all these jobs, she would have never been able to afford that. Plus, the only way Gina would be able to make those types of decisions for Michael was if she was his legal guardian, which may have been plausible under the circumstances. But Michael said he went to private boarding school on a ranch in Texas. That doesn't make sense. Didn't he say that he had always lived in California? He met DJ and his family there. DJ said his parents loved him so much, he thought they adopted him. Michael is like a son, and DJ is the big brother. What's wrong with this story? So what happened after he left Marysville? Furthermore, who is Gina, and what was her role in this?*

Chapter 42

Sera and Michael were in their usual meditation pose, sitting cross-legged, facing each other and holding hands by the pool. Anni was quietly observing them from the lanai above and had to admit she was mesmerized. Sera had made some type of herbal tea, which she insisted Michael drink several times a day. Part of what fascinated her was that Michael followed her lead, never once questioning her. Then, they went through some sort of prayer or chant together. A healing prayer. She heard Sera tell him: "Cancer is caused by a spiritual disharmony within you. Whatever has caused this for you, you have to release it, Michael."

He bowed his head. "I don't know if I can, Sera."

"I'm not asking you to forgive. I'm asking you to release whatever the pain is that you are holding onto, because it's hurting your soul."

"I want to, but I'm not sure I can do that. Some pain is too deep."

Sera was patient with him. "Okay, Michael. Let's go back to the first lesson. You have your guardian angels and spiritual guides. Guardian angels watch over and protect you. They have been with you even before you were born. Spiritual guides are with you on earth and are sages, old souls who have much wisdom and love for you. They know everything about you. They are here to offer you messages and, in times of stress, can comfort you."

"How do I ask my guide for help? I don't want to be sick anymore."

"The calmer you are, the more you will be able to hear their messages for you. If you ask them three times in a row, they will know you are serious and pay attention. Remember, they want to help you. It pleases them to offer you assistance." She squeezed his hands. "Now, start by thanking your angels and guides for their love. Then ask for a sign on how to release this emotional baggage you don't need to carry anymore."

"Are you one of my spiritual guides, Sera?"

"There are teachers and healers. I was sent to teach."

"Can you heal me?"

"Healing and curing is not the same thing. You can heal yourself."

"While I don't understand all of this, I'll have faith you know what to do. That's part of loving you."

"You don't have to understand it all, you just have to believe that the universe will support you when you let go of whatever is making you sick." Tenderly, she lifted his face toward her. "And I love you too, Michael."

He took a deep breath. "I've held onto this for years, and telling you this, makes me feel so small and helpless. I hate that feeling."

"Let it go, Michael." Sera encouraged him.

Anni was afraid to move, fearful they would realize she had been sitting there all along, and also not wanting to disrupt the moment. But at the same time she felt like she was invading their privacy. Closing her eyes, she said one of the little prayers she had heard Sera teach Michael. *I will act with good intention, to help, and not cause harm to my brother. Let the wind carry my love to those in need . . .* the only thing she heard in the wind was Michael, and she could sense the raw emotion in his voice.

Sera was as still as the pool behind them. She had learned not to absorb the pain of others, but to deflect it, letting it scatter on the wind. Empathy could come later, but this was not what Michael needed right now. Her role was to facilitate releasing whatever was causing the pain, and that could only be done by the person feeling it. Healing would be the next step. He was still holding her hands, and she could feel him trembling and it made her feel jittery inside. Gently, she let go and began to feel calmer inside. She spoke softly: "What are you feeling right now?"

"I've spent most of my life feeling angry. I never had a father. When I was little, I'd see these fathers and kids playing together, but the only thing I did was watch and wonder what that would be like. Actually, I was jealous and lonely.

"As you know, I was pretty much raised by Gina. She was kind to me, but she couldn't protect me from the wrath of the woman who called herself my mother, which, by the way, isn't even the truth. Gina got into trouble with drugs when she was sixteen and got pregnant. I'm the product of that mess.

"I only know that because I overheard Gina and Claire fighting, and Claire was screaming at Gina and calling her awful names. Gina was trying to take care of me and finish school. Claire didn't want to be saddled with me. I always felt like a burden instead of a bundle of joy."

Michael stopped and took a deep breath. "When Gina wasn't there, Claire was mean to me. Honestly, I was scared to death of her." He stopped again, and lowered his head, choking back a sob. "I'll just say she hurt me. There were times I hid from her . . ." He spaced out on her, lost in memories.

Little Michael was home from first grade with the flu, curled up in a blanket on the sofa. First, he was burning up, then he had chills. Gina wasn't home, and Claire was in charge. His stomach was churning. Honestly, he tried to make it to the bathroom, but it was too late, and he vomited all over the floor. When Claire saw what had happened, she yelled at him: "You're always making work for me. I did not sign up for this job, you little bastard."

She brought in a bucket of soapy water and paper towels. "Clean it up. It's your mess." Crawling off the sofa, he got down on his hands and knees and cleaned up the floor. The entire time she stood, looming over him screaming. "You insufferable piece of shit." Next, he lugged the bucket to the bathroom and poured everything down the toilet.

"Now, take the bucket and go to your room. If you're going to puke again, do it in the bucket." Wordlessly, he started for his room. She grabbed him by the arm, jerking him around to face her. Her voice was

cold and hard as steel. "One more thing, you need to wash your hands. You're a dirty boy."

Turning around, he walked toward the sink. "Here, Michael." She pointed to the toilet. "That's your punishment. Wash your hands in the toilet. Don't make me mad again or next time I'll spank you until you can't sit down for a week."

He started to whimper, trying not to cry in front of her, because crying really set her off. Even worse, his stomach was churning again, threatening to erupt. He didn't know what to do. Fortunately, this time he managed to hit the toilet. Only a little bit of vomit landed on the floor . . . and on her shoe. He grabbed some toilet paper and hurriedly tried to clean it up before she saw it. But it was too late.

This time, she kicked him in the backside. He doubled over. Seizing him by a leg, she literally drug him out of the bathroom on his stomach, then picked him up and hurled him onto his bed. Slamming the bucket down, she leered at him, "If you say one word of this to Gina, I swear to God I will punish you in ways you can't even imagine. Do you hear me?"

She grabbed him by his face, screaming, so close she was spitting in his face. "Do you hear me?" Meekly, he nodded, choking back tears. He heard her and believed her.

Sera touched his arm and he jumped as if someone had just hit him with a stun gun. "Where did you just go?"

Michael looked dazed. "What? I'm sorry."

"You said Claire hurt you?"

"Oh. Yeah." He still looked faraway. "Gina would ask me how I got hurt, and I thought if I told her, Claire would probably kill me. Finally, a teacher at school suspected something was wrong at home, and children's services came and that was the first time I was taken away." He sighed.

"Actually, that was one of my better years, because they cared for me, and finally, I didn't have to worry about what was going to happen to me tomorrow. But then I was returned back to Claire's house. For a while, things were better. Everything was pretty good when Claire was in another hospital. Gina was getting a degree in music, and we spent a lot of time together. Then Claire came home.

She was decent enough as long as she stayed on her medication, but it never lasted. When she blew up, it was like a tornado struck the house. I think Gina was scared of her, too."

Michael rubbed his temples as if he had a massive headache. "For some reason I'll never understand, that woman hated me and I became the brunt of her rages. Once again, I was shuffled off to foster care. In total, I think that happened four times. But after I hit about twelve years old, I started getting sent off to these boy's ranches. I was really homesick there. These places were almost worse than living with Claire. I couldn't relate at all with the other kids there, and got bullied by the bigger guys. Kids there had gotten into trouble with drugs or legal issues. To them, I was just this lightweight. So mostly I stayed to myself and tried to stay out of trouble. Believe it or not, I just wanted to go home."

"You never told me any of this. Why, Michael?"

"I was too embarrassed. I didn't want anyone to know."

Sera took his hand again. "What happened next?"

"Eventually, I got to go back home. I was so happy to see Gina. She said we were moving to a place called Marysville. She had gotten a job there, and the courts determined her life stable enough for me to come home. But you know how that turned out, and I got sent away again. This time I never came back, but I didn't want to see Gina anymore. I hated her for sending me away again."

"Were you angry with Gina or in the circumstances?"

"First, I was angry with Gina because she couldn't protect me. But then, it just seemed I was always the one being punished and sent away. That really hurt more than Claire smacking me around."

"What happened after you left Marysville?"

"At first, Gina sent me to another one of those unbearable ranches. There was like a chain of them, and I got transferred from California to Texas. I was absolutely lost. I focused on keeping my grades up and kept studying music. Music was my therapy. At night, I barricaded myself in my room. Bad things can happen in those places, and I felt really vulnerable. At some point, I realized my only salvation was getting out of there any way I could. That meant I could either commit suicide or run away."

"What did you choose, Michael?"

"I chose to run away, and I almost made it."

"Then what?"

"They had hearings about what they referred to as incidences. This caught the attention of a woman on the board of directors who requested a full review of my situation. She was kind enough to call Gina and arranged a meeting with me and Gina. We talked for over two hours. She said I didn't belong in such a place, as I wasn't a troubled kid, and made arrangements to send me to a private boarding school. Her name was Marilee Jansen, and she saved me."

"DJ's mother?"

Michael nodded. "They were amazing. She felt sorry for me and thought I deserved an opportunity. Gina signed over legal guardianship, and they sort of took over parenting me. DJ and I met at school, and at first, I wasn't sure he liked me. But we got to know each other, and he became like an older brother to me."

"So what is your relationship with them today?"

"As you know, I wouldn't be where I am today without them. To say I'm grateful would be an understatement. Of course, we're all very busy, and DJ's father is all business. But I talk to them at least once a month and try to go visit them a couple times a year. Of course, in between there are always business meetings to attend, and I catch up with DJ's dad there. And I'm on the board of directors for that ranch, so that if another kid gets stuck in that jail, I can help save someone like me."

"That's wonderful of you. So who or what are you still angry with in your life?"

"I'm mostly angry at Gina. She was my mother, and she dumped me like a stray dog at the pound. I couldn't imagine doing that to my Rose. Not to mention, crazy Claire got to stay at home. I think someone should have locked her up and lost the key."

"Let's look at from another perspective." Sera treaded lightly. "Gina was a child that had a baby. Her mother never loved her, so she had no compass for how to mother you. I don't know this, but can you imagine the abuse Gina probably endured as a little girl growing up with a mother with mental illness. Gina did the best she could, and out of love for you, she sent you away. Can you imagine how she must have felt when people kept taking you away from her because she couldn't be a decent mother? In a final act of love, she gave legal custody to a family she didn't even know. I think her actions today are guided by terrible guilt about the life you had. That's the real reason she acts the way she does. She's trying to make it up to you.'

Michael was quiet, mulling over what Sera said. "I've always pushed her away. That must hurt her. I'm punishing her."

"Now that you understand, does it help you to release being angry at her? Can you see her, not as your mother, but as a scared little girl that did the best she could under what sounds like some pretty terrible circumstances?"

"It makes me feel sad for her. I never thought of her as a victim, too."

Sera smiled. "Here is the good news. You don't have to do that anymore. So are you ready to release that now?"

Michael smiled back. "I'll release it because I know it's the right thing to do, but I can't forgive and forget."

Anni laid her head on her arm and closed her eyes. It all made sense now. It wasn't so much a great mystery as it was a monumental burden. She thought back to their conversation on the jet when they were flying to Maui. Michael was quick to sympathize with her. Now she understood why. It was like all pieces of a puzzle suddenly connected. If she had simply asked, he might have told her. She needed to explain this to Joe. It seemed important that Joe should know this piece.

Chapter 43

"Who wants to go to Vegas?" Michael was in an upbeat mood.

Anni balked. "I don't think that's a good idea. Your white counts may still be low."

"Well, I'm tired of being sick. Let's go have some fun. Just for the weekend." He turned to DJ. "Can you fly us?"

"Sure." DJ stood up. "It's what I do best."

Sera joined the conversation. "Fly airplanes?"

He winked at her. "No, party."

Chapter 44

Joe heard his cell phone ringing. Rolling over, he closed his eyes. It must be a wrong number. Who could possibly be calling in the middle of the night? The phone continued to demand that he answer. Whoever was trying to reach him was certainly persistent. Opening one eye, he glanced at the clock on the nightstand: 3:00 a.m. *Seriously?* "Hello," he mumbled groggily.

"Is this Joe di Blasio?"

"I think so."

"It's Seraphine. Michael has collapsed."

Joe was suddenly wide awake. "Where are you?"

"DJ is flying us into Marysville. Meet us at the airport."

Stars glittered against a black velvet night. Joe looked at his watch again. A half hour had gone by since Sera's call. Shivering, he searched the frigid night sky for any sign of life. Ten minutes later, he saw a bright light, slicing through the night, advancing toward the airport. DJ gently eased *Touch & Go* onto the short runway. Joe made his way to the jet.

Sera was cradling Michael in her lap, gently stroking his forehead. His face was flushed.

"What happened?" asked Joe.

Anni answered him. "Michael had insisted on going to Las Vegas for the weekend. He said he wanted his life back. I advised him not to go, but he wouldn't listen. The weekend went well, and he seemed all right. We had boarded the jet and had just taken off to fly back home and that's when he flipped out. He was trying the doors and talking total nonsense. Finally, I got him to lie down. He feels really hot. I think he spiked a fever."

"Let's get him to the hospital."

Michael peered up at Joe without a glimmer of recognition. "I'm trying to find the red slippers. Do you know where they are?"

"Let's go. DJ, stay in the backseat with him. Don't let him near a door, please."

DJ attempted to make sense. "When we were in Las Vegas, he seemed fine. I don't know what the fuck happened, but I diverted Marysville. I had to get out of the air. I can't have someone popping open a door and taking a trip to Oz."

Joe and Sera sat beside Michael all night. His fever had peaked at 104. Sera placed compresses on his forehead, cooling him with tepid sponges. He was delirious: *"Come to daddy, Rose. Dial down, DJ, I can't keep up . . . Ah gee . . . it snowed in Maui . . . No, don't touch me . . ."*

Ironically, he was in the same room as before. Once again, security flanked the doors.

Michael felt something soft and wet touching his face. Nice, soothing. Blackness engulfed him, and he descended into a place where sleep was the only option. He stayed there until he heard the beeping of a machine.

"Joe?"

"Welcome back, Michael."

"Where am I?"

"Marysville."

"I hate this town. How did I get here?"

"You were running a high fever and hallucinating. Dr. Poddy is on his way. He'll be here in the morning."

Michael turned to Sera. "Am I going to be okay?"

"We're not sure what happened." Sera attempted to sound calm, but her expression gave her away.

They had unanimously decided not to tell him about the reporters swarming in the lobby. DJ was desperately trying to gloss over last night's events. It seems a reporter had somehow found out their destination was Marysville. Someone dispatched a photographer and now incriminating photos of Michael being carried into the hospital were splattered all over the Internet. This, coupled with DJ's announcement that their upcoming tour was cancelled had created a firestorm.

Chapter 45

Dr. Poddy arrived about the same time as Gina. Of course, everyone had stayed the night so they could be beside him in the morning. The doctor went straight to the point. "Labs indicate your white count is elevated. In short, you have pneumonia. Most likely, you contracted this as a result of chemotherapy. At any rate, I'm going to have you placed in isolation and start some IV antibiotics. You should be feeling much better in a few days, but for the next six months I don't want you traveling. Anywhere. Once you recover, go home and stay there. Do you understand what I'm saying?"

Michael looked like a scolded kid, his face was crimson. "Got it. I apologize. I'm not a good patient."

"When your white count is low, you are at high risk for infection. Award ceremonies and road trips are out. By the way, congratulations on the award, though I have no idea where you got the energy to perform. If your white counts come down, you can go home in the next couple days." He turned to Anni, who was crumpled in a corner of the room. "You are his private duty nurse. See to it that he behaves."

Gina turned, glaring at her. "If I had known this at the awards ceremony, I would have personally fired you. You are in charge of his care. If anything like this happens again, I'll be taking care of him in Maui."

Michael shook his head. "It's not her fault. I was going to that ceremony if DJ had to carry me. She tried to tell me not to go to, but I went anyway, you know me, I'm stubborn."

Gina lit on Anni first. "Is that true?" Then back to Michael, "Stubborn can kill you."

Anni ran from the room.

Joe followed and found her crying in the hallway.

"This is all my fault. I should have forced him to stay home."

"You honestly think you have that power? He would have gone anyway." Joe put his arm around her.

"It doesn't matter. I failed him. He's sick because of me."

Joe took her by the arms. "He's going to be fine. Michael isn't angry with you. His oncologist probably told him not to travel, but he never mentioned it to you. You weren't with him for the last chemo treatment."

"I should have known his white count was low and made him stay home."

"You know now." Joe gave her a hug. A camera flashed. "Hey, how did reporters get up here?"

Security swarmed the guy. The reporter was dressed in a white lab coat. He was promptly escorted out of the hospital.

* * *

For the time being, Gina had velcroed herself to Michael's side. "You haven't touched your breakfast."

"Look at it, Gina. Would you eat it? I'm not even sure what it is."

"It's oatmeal, I think. Do you want me to get something else for you?"

"I just want to go home."

Sera was sitting quietly, watching the scene before her. Her thoughts went back to the walk on the beach with Anni. *How long would Michael tolerate her fussing over him?*

"Why don't you stay with me for a while?" suggested Gina.

"That would be impossible. The press would converge like it was a crime scene."

There was a knock at the door, and Dr. Poddy stepped inside, with Anni close behind.

Sera sighed. *Now we will never know . . .*

Michael pulled himself to full stature as if he were bracing himself for whatever came next. Dr. Poddy was not the type that minced words. "The X-ray was clear. No signs of infection. And since you're in remission . . ."

"I'm in remission? Are you serious? Remission?"

"Yes, which means we are now at the stage of watchful waiting."

"But that's good news, right? No more chemotherapy?"

"No more chemo, Michael. But we will need to continue to monitor you. For now, I'd like monthly labs and another X-ray in another three months. I meant what I said about going home and resting. Anyway, I'm discharging you. You can go home tomorrow morning."

Sera gave him a hug and whispered something in his ear, so Gina couldn't hear her. He smiled broadly and kissed her on the cheek. Gina rolled her eyes and left the room.

Chapter 46

The elevator stopped at first floor, cardiac. Second floor, maternity. Third floor, rock & roll. She was met by a battalion of security guards. Gloria stepped off the elevator. "My goodness, a welcoming committee! I'm here to see Michael Dolanski."

Sera was coming down the hall and stopped to listen.

"Excuse me . . . " Security stopped her. "But you would need a pass to visit patients on this floor. Do you have some sort of identification?"

"I believe my husband is here. I need a pass to see my husband?"

"I'm sorry, but if you were the president's wife, you'd need a pass to be here." Security didn't budge.

"Tell him Gloria is here. I came all the way from LA, and I expect to see him."

"Check her out while I find out if Mr. Dolanski is expecting a wife."

Sera stepped into Michael's room, closing the door. "Are you expecting company?"

Michael frowned. "What is it? Is something wrong, Sera?"

"Kind of, Michael. Your wife is here?"

* * *

DJ opened the door, but said nothing. Gina and Sera stayed close by.

Gloria gushed into the room, "I've been so worried about you. All this news about you collapsing and the rumors that you are seriously ill. What is the matter with you?"

Michael was impenetrable. "What brings you to my bedside? I'm surprised you knew the way."

Gina spoke through clenched teeth. "She probably caught a northerly wind and blew this way on her broomstick." She nodded to DJ. He nodded back, smiling slightly. Michael quickly glanced at both of them and smirked.

Gloria ignored them and continued. "Michael, sweetheart, you look dreadful." She sat down next to him on the bed. "What happened? All this drama for a simple virus?"

Michael never took his eyes off her. "Well, it started with losing all my money in Vegas, which might be bad news for you. Then I don't know, after that, I was just a psychotic mess. Where's Rose?"

"Very funny, Michael. You don't ever gamble when it comes to money. She's at home, with our new nanny. You know, the new spy you hired."

"So now we can add paranoid to your list of character defects?" Michael shook his head, sighing. "Why can't we make nice for Rose?"

She had placed her hand on his leg, gently massaging his leg as if she were feeling up Hansel or Gretel for the oven. "What's your definition of nice?"

"I meant that it would be easier on Rose if we were cooperative. I don't want to be known as nothing more than a monthly check in the mail. I think she needs to know we both love her."

"You don't want anything to do with me, but you love Rose?"

"Why does that seem unusual to you? I only want her to know that we both love her, that I love her."

"Whatever is wrong with you must have affected your mind." She quit rubbing his leg.

Michael pulled back. "I can't imagine you came all the way here for a friendly visit. Did you not receive your check? That could have been handled by a simple text message."

"Forgive me for caring."

Catch a Falling Star

"Forgive me for not trusting you." He motioned to his friends. "I have witnesses."

"I only wanted to make sure you are going to be okay. I wanted to see you for myself. You know, you can't truly know if the news is reliable. Of course, the *National Tattler* has reported that you are seriously ill. But that could just be a publicity stunt, misinformation, or nothing at all. So I decided there was only one way to know for sure. Come here and see you for myself."

"Translation." Michael forced a tight smile. "You want to make sure your benefactor isn't about to cancel his subscriptions?"

"What would you like me to tell them?" Gloria put a vice grip on his leg and he flinched away.

"Why would you assume it is your responsibility to speak in my behalf? Especially since you don't have a clue, which would mean anything you say could be considered slander."

"If there is nothing to tell, why the secrets?"

"There are no secrets. You need to leave. You are trying my patience, and that's not good since I don't have any of that left." Michael motioned to Gina. "Escort her out. I just cancelled her visiting pass."

"Feel better. I'll tell Rose you will be coming by soon. And I'm not worried. You know what they say, only the good die young." Gloria breezed past Sera on a sea of perfumed hair.

DJ finally spoke, holding up his phone. "Got it all on video. Thanks for the sign, Gina."

Gina smiled. "Isn't technology a wonderful thing?"

* * *

Anni was about to check on Michael when she was almost flattened to the floor as Gloria slammed out of the room.

"I demand to speak with his nurse." Gloria was like a spitting cobra.

"I'm his nurse, Anni Cavatini. May I help you?"

"I want to speak with you. Privately."

Anni steeled herself. "Right here, right now. What do you want?"

Gloria was breathing as if she had just finished a marathon. "I don't have time to play games with you. We have a daughter together. I have to protect her." She turned on Sera. "Who are you? What are you doing here? He has girls as bodyguards now?"

Anni took her by the arm. "Come with me to my office. No one goes in there unless I clear it with Michael."

Once her office door closed, Anni turned on her. "I'm shocked at your behavior. There are privacy laws. You cannot charge in here and demand confidential information. If he wanted you to know anything, he would tell you."

"I gather he is quite ill. That's what he told me."

"I have no idea what he did or did not tell you."

"I'm not some stupid reporter."

"You're also not his wife." Anni was not about to back down. "I can march down there right now and ask him what he told you. You don't intimidate me, Gloria." She opened her office door, "Get out." Stepping into the hallway, she beckoned to security. "Escort her out of the hospital. If she tries to come back, then we will have her arrested."

Chapter 47

"**I hear we have good news.**"

Michael opened his eyes and smiled at Joe. "Where have you been hiding all day?"

"Student nurses."

"Shame on you." He pushed himself up on one elbow. "Are any of them pretty?"

"That's what they keep asking me about you."

"Well, what do you tell them?"

"I tell them the truth. There is only one Michael Dolanski, and I have his cell number. They like me." Joe paused. "By the way, you were looking for red slippers?"

Michael laughed. "I said that? DJ and I always say we need a pair of ruby slippers when we're tired and want to go home." He added, "Hey, I'm going home in the morning."

"Yes, I heard. *Touch & Go* is ready to take you there."

"I'll miss you, Joe."

"I don't think so. I'm going with you. I've made my decision."

* * *

It happened that simply. Joe moved to the guest room in the loft next to Anni. They shared the private lanai, Jacuzzi and caught up on lost time. Basically, they lived in a luxurious penthouse with an ocean view.

"Joe, do you ever feel like you've died and this is heaven?"

"This may be the closest I ever get to heaven."

Anni laughed. "You're always so serious. Michael said it is now mandatory that we have some fun. They have invited us to go out to dinner with them tonight."

"Sounds like fun. Actually, I'm looking forward to, well, looking forward."

"Really? That has to be a new experience for you." She kissed him on the cheek. "I think I'm going to like the new you. Come to think of it, I already do like you. A lot."

* * *

"What is this place, DJ? I've never heard of the Cellar." Michael took off his sunglasses, frowning.

"It's one of those off-the-path places. I've been here several times and promise fans won't find us here."

"What kind of prehistoric specialties do they serve in this cave?"

"Not cave, the Cellar. Besides I'm in the mood for some down home cooking."

Michael glanced over his shoulder to Joe and Anni. Sera rested on his arm. "That means something burnt-over mesquite and Mexican beer served in paper cups. It's not too late to develop the norovirus, which we all might get anyway if we eat here."

"Trust me, Michael. It's safe." DJ patted him on the back.

Two middle-aged women waltzed in wearing Balinese sarongs, big floppy hats, and oversized sunglasses.

Michael frowned. "What's that, DJ? Catch of the day?"

DJ was laughing. "If you're going to act like a big baby, go sit in the car and pout by yourself." DJ turned to the group. "He's been here before. He's just trying to block it out."

"I swear to God, I've never seen this place. I'm sure I'd remember it, DJ."

They found a secluded table in the corner near the patio and settled in. Anni liked the ambience. It reminded her of the coffee houses back in her college days. Folk art and poetry graced the walls. There was even a jukebox, though at the moment nothing was playing. They sat quietly for about ten minutes. When no waiter showed up, Michael motioned to DJ.

"Do they have menus, or do you just have to take whatever they bring to the table?"

"I have connections. I know the chef." DJ hurried away.

Resting his chin in his hand, Michael smiled at them. "I think I have amazing tolerance."

Sera smiled back. "He has connections. I'm sure we're fine."

About then, DJ surfaced with a waitress dressed in a Hawaiian skirt and halter top. "What'll it be tonight, Mr. DJ?"

"How about armadillo on the half shell for everyone?" DJ was in a rare, playful mood.

"None for me, thanks." Joe passed.

"I'll have to pass on that too." Sera joined in the camaraderie.

"Whatever you serve, just make sure Mr. DJ gets the bill." Michael turned to his buddy. "I thought you said this was a place where people didn't know your name?"

"They don't know your name. I'm infamous here." DJ was hugging the waitress. "Bring us all a round of beer. You know what I like."

"Got it." The waitress wandered toward the bar, then paused. "That's the one with the orange slices, right?"

Michael smiled. "You're pathetic."

DJ added, "In case you haven't noticed, Michael has now started the two-word sentence game."

Michael shook his head. "Not true."

"See, he just did it." DJ was laughing. "Unless he wants something, then he gets real . . . what's that big word, Michael?"

"I'm right?"

"If that means bossy and stubborn, then yes." The beer arrived, and DJ seemed to be enjoying more of it than anyone else. "It's a game we invented in school to annoy our teachers."

Michael laughed. "And it worked. They hated us. We were obnoxious."

DJ nodded. "God, we had fun, didn't we?"

"Well, if you think pissing off people is fun, I guess so." Michael smiled. "Though, I kind of got tired of sitting in the counselor's office."

Sera enjoyed watching them, but sat back, listening. This was a part of Michael's life she knew nothing about. At least, it sounded better than his earlier years, and for that, she was grateful. Under the table, she gently squeezed his hand. He squeezed back.

Anni jumped up, plugging some change into the jukebox. Using her own two-word sentence, she laughed, "You're on." She had picked two songs from their band.

DJ grabbed two knives and started drumming. Michael stood and started to sing along with himself. DJ joined in the refrain. Anni was dancing, and when Michael joined her on the floor, it became an impromptu concert. Then something snapped, and Joe wasn't sure how, but he found himself next to Anni and Michael on the dance floor. He knew the words of the song because he had listened to it a thousand times before, alone in his car and in his apartment. This time he sang along with Michael. As for Sera, she enjoyed the moment and just prayed for more to come.

Michael turned to Joe and smiled, "You bastard."

Joe had his own two words: "My mentor."

They both laughed.

Chapter 48

It was almost noon when Joe heard muffled laughter by the pool. Punching the button on the remote, the glass wall glided open to the cabana. Michael and DJ waved him over to the cafe. Michael handed him a frosty glass.

"What is this?"

"I have no idea what I've been drinking, but I feel wonderful." He took a tiny sip. "Whatever it is, it's good."

DJ was swigging it down, "I say we tell him now."

"Tell me what?" Joe frowned.

"We're going on tour for three months. Bye-bye Maui."

"When are you leaving?"

DJ put his arm around him, "The question is not when we are leaving, but how soon can you pack."

"Why am I going?"

Michael cocked his head. "Why do you look like someone that just lost all his money in a casino?"

Joe objected. "But what can I do? Why do you need me?"

"To put it simply," DJ smiled. "You are on Team Dolanski. Michael wants you there."

"What about Anni? Is she going on tour?"

They looked at each other. Michael spoke, "I'm not sick anymore, so I don't need a nurse. Besides, Sera will be with me. You have work to do."

* * *

Joe was pouting. "I can't believe I'm going and you're not. He needs you more than he needs me."

Anni tried not to laugh at him. "I think Michael is usually about two steps ahead of everyone else. It's fine with me, honestly. I'll stay. You go on tour. I envy you. I'd love to see how they work and play."

"I'm not cut out for road trips."

"If the Pope can do it, so can you."

"But I'll miss you."

"I hate that part, too, but we'll stay in touch, okay?"

"Can't you convince him you should go?"

"I seriously doubt anyone persuades Michael of much, unless he wants to be convinced." Kissing him, she added, "I'm a homebody. This suits me just fine. If Michael needs me for any reason, I know he or DJ will call."

"Okay, I guess."

"Lighten up. You can finally tell everyone you're officially with the band."

"I'll bring you a T-shirt."

Hugging him, she added. "I have to see if absence really does make the heart grow fonder or if it's just a myth. Besides, I have a couple of things on my 'to do' list."

"I'm assuming I'm not on that list?"

"You get a three-month sabbatical. Enjoy it." She paused. "On another subject, I overheard a conversation between Michael and Sera. I think it's important that you hear this." Anni gave him the complete unedited version.

Joe listened patiently. "I knew Gina was his mother." He explained what happened in the chapel and about giving her back the blue baby bracelet. "But I've never heard the rest of the story. Michael has eluded to a troubled childhood. It explains a lot for me. Thank you for sharing."

Anni nodded. "I thought you should know."

Chapter 49

In the meantime, Joe had no idea what being on the road meant. The band had a publicity manager that travelled with them and told everyone where to be, what to say, what not to do, and there were no exceptions. Every time they landed in a new city, their crew set up the stage. Michael and DJ were constantly doing interviews or on late night TV shows, promoting the tour. Quite frankly, he rarely saw them, and when he did, they were either coming or going someplace else.

Basically, his duties consisted of making sure they had everything they needed and everyone stayed on task. Dry cleaning picked up, fresh fruit in their rooms, no smoking zones near Michael. It was a far cry from being a priest. He also took notes on the crowds' reactions.

Every show had the same playlist and was always played like they had never performed before tonight. They would be in eighteen cities between February and mid-April, starting with the Fillmore in Denver and ending with the Blaisdell in Honolulu.

He never saw drugs or wild parties. If it was happening, it was far away from him. What he did see was lots of teamwork. When he did catch a glimpse of DJ and Michael, they looked tired. Another one of his new responsibilities was to monitor their websites, Twitter account and reviews posted during and after each show. The next morning there was always a debriefing.

"How are we doing, Joe?"

"Let's see, last night we were in Mashantucket, Connecticut. Fans loved it when you went into the crowd, and everyone got up and sang with you, Michael. There are lots tweets about how easily you relate with every age group. Great backup band, not overpowering, they loved the sequence of the songs and the energy in the arena. Of course, they love Michael's dance moves, his ad lib comments with the audience and camaraderie with the band. A true professional, relaxed, playful, sexy, and not bad to look at. This one woman said she thinks her husband has a man crush on you."

Michael scrunched up his face. "I didn't need that last comment. Any criticisms?"

"The concert lasted about an hour and fifteen minutes. As always, they wanted more time with you. Oh, and one tweet asked if you could start with your latest hit and end with it, too. I guess they really like that number."

DJ nodded. "We've heard that one before. What should we do?"

Both Michael and DJ turned to their manager.

He was a no-nonsense kind of guy but very respectful to everyone. "No. We stick with the current playlist." He turned to the group. "In two days, we're in Madison Square Garden. We're at the halfway mark. No changes."

* * *

There was one night that Joe remembered more than any of the others: San Francisco.

Gina was there. She had come earlier in the day and stayed all night. It was the first time he ever saw her let loose, laughing and dancing, absolutely enjoying the moment. Michael had her come onstage with him and introduced her as the first woman he ever loved. Very nice. But that wasn't the part he remembered.

Chapter 50

Gloria wasn't one to give up without a fight, so it made perfect sense she opted for Plan B. Of course, Michael provided her and Rose with medical insurance. She dialed the number on the back of her card. "I have several claims for Michael Dolanski. I need to speak to someone who can explain this to me."

Her call was transferred. "May I help you?"

"There are several claims here for my husband. Can you clarify what we are responsible for? I'm sorry. He asked me to call in his behalf. He isn't feeling well. I can provide you with his social security number."

"Please, yes."

Gloria provided Michael's information, praising herself for keeping it from their years of living together.

"I'm not showing any outstanding claims, Mrs. Dolanski. His surgery has been paid in full."

"Are you referencing his hospitalization in Marysville?"

"Well, yes. He was there twice. Both have been covered. The only claims I have listed that have not been paid yet are for his last chemotherapy treatment. Is there a problem?"

"I think so. The chemotherapy. That would be standard, not experimental, right?"

"I'm unable to determine that by looking at the claims, though you may want to verify that with his doctor."

"Thank you. I will do that."

"Of course, you are aware. We are prohibited by privacy laws to share personal information."

"Thank you so much."

"Is there anything more I can do to help you?"

"I don't think I caught your name?"

"Cindy."

"Thank you, Cindy. If I have any more questions, I'll ask for you."

* * *

Michael gave Gina a final hug before she left the stage and the band kicked off the second half of the show. The first couple songs were pure hot, climactic fun. The next set was a series of love songs. Michael made his way off stage and into the crowd. Incidentally, this was simultaneous with their manager always having a mini heart attack, even though security guards were everywhere. But Michael always seemed right at home, letting fans hug and kiss him. He hugged them back, and they danced and sang along with him.

And then he did it. Walking back to the stage, he stopped, turning to Seraphine, who was standing out of sight, watching from backstage. Smiling, he took her hand and led her back to the stage with him.

Their manager whispered aloud, "Come on, Michael. Make it count."

Standing before her, he took both of her hands, and began singing one of the first love songs he had ever written. Every wedding planner in America added the ballad to their playlist. In the silence, Joe could hear every woman there stop breathing. When the song ended, Michael spoke to his fans, but mostly he spoke to Sera. "Everyone deserves to be loved. If you love someone, tell them tonight. You may never get another chance."

The audience went insane. When the song finished, Michael whispered into Sera's ear. "Never again will I send you running into the night."

She cried, but they were tears of joy. "I will stand strong by your side. I never stopped loving you." Softly, he kissed her hands.

The reviews were the best they had ever seen.

That night Joe called Anni. When it went to voicemail, he left the following message. "I need to let you know how much I love you. I just needed to say that tonight. I love you, Anni. Two more weeks and I'll be home."

* * *

That night, Sera cradled him in her arms. "It's been such a long time, but it feels like yesterday."

He stroked her hair away so he could fully see her face. "I don't know why you love me? I've hardly given you a reason."

"Love doesn't need a reason. It's what I feel in my heart." She touched his chest. "Here, Michael."

"I am so sorry, Sera." Tenderly, he kissed her on the forehead. "I wasn't there for you."

"You weren't able. I've always been here for you, but the timing wasn't right. It was supposed to be now. This moment."

He felt like he wanted to cry. "I've never felt like this with anyone, Sera. I'm overwhelmed by your love for me."

She began unbuttoning his shirt. "Please, Michael, love me tonight. I know you've been putting this off because you are afraid . . ."

"After surgery, physically, I don't know if I can . . ."

"Whatever happens is okay. I'll stay." Her fingers delicately flickered down his neck, then on to his shoulders. "Open your eyes, Michael. Look at me."

He felt vulnerable, no longer in control. Ironically, he felt safe with her and wanted her to take control of him. He submitted to her. She slipped off his clothes, then tossed her clothes to the floor. In silence, she began stroking his hair and face. He relented, with nothing more than a whimper. Once again, Sera was taken back to her first experiences with Michael.

Patiently, she caressed him, lavishing his chest with light, airy kisses. Her hands easily glided further. She could feel his body tensing and backing off a little, until she could hear him breathing deeply, moaning softly as she went further down on him, tasting him, playing with him.

"Oh my god." Michael pulled her so close that he could feel his heart beating against her breasts. He began to give back to her, nibbling her ears and teasing her with his tongue until she gasped. He couldn't stand holding back. It was like the very first time, and he was so aroused, he could barely wait.

His hands were soft but forceful against her thighs, pressing her legs apart . . . she needed to feel his strength as he slid into a place he hadn't been in years. Sera was immersed in the moment, taken back to years ago, as he said, "Yes I can, Sera."

"Then giddy up, Michael." They both laughed at their childish terms.

He pressed so hard that she cried out with both pain and pleasure. This was far removed from a little game he had invented to full domination. Pulling her into him, he took control of her, gently holding her down, and she enjoyed submitting completely. She felt released from needing to be in charge and almost felt dizzy from his intensity. She had lost count of the nights she had dreamed of this moment again.

For Michael, it was a huge sense of relief. All of his senses were totally in tune with her, and as they both hit their peak together, he knew he couldn't have stopped himself if he had tried. He was overwhelmed by her sensual scent, her beauty, and her passion, and gave in to her every whim, wanting to please her in every possible way that he could.

When they were done, he chuckled softly. It was a new game he had personally invented. She felt giddy from the moment.

Afterward, Michael buried his face in her hair. "Tell me you'll stay, Sera. You're not leaving me."

"How could I let you go? You are connected to my soul."

"So you will stay?" Michael turned her face toward him.

"I dare you to try and get rid of me." She was mounted on top of him, smiling.

"Ahh . . . " He sighed. "Take me home. You can do whatever you want with me. I'm yours."

Gently, Sera began massaging him. "Be afraid, Michael."

He laughed. "Why should I be afraid? You're the one in danger of being loved to death?"

Chapter 51

DJ ambled toward the kitchen. It was almost noon. Perhaps some caffeine would perk him up. Evidently someone was up, because he could smell coffee brewing.

"Anni? Joe?" He spied Sera, perched cross-legged on a chair. He was still trying to get used to this new addition to the family.

"Good morning." Sera handed him a mug. "Late night party?"

"That's where it started. Where is everyone?" He poured himself some coffee.

"Anni went shopping for groceries. When I last saw Joe, he was talking to someone on his phone."

"This isn't a home, it's a hotel." DJ sighed. "Where is Michael hiding?"

"He went to see Rose. Michael didn't want to subject me to Gloria, so I stayed here."

"One of these days, Gloria and Michael are going to kill each other." DJ drank half a cup and poured some more coffee into his mug. "Anyway, you can thank him for leaving you here. She has a way of bringing out the worst in him. How's Michael?"

"He's all right. Sometimes a little moody, but he's dealing with a lot emotionally. I understand him. I know how to handle him."

DJ chuckled. "That would be something to see. Your confidence is either inspiring or delusional. But I have to admit, I've never seen Michael as content as he is with you. I'm glad you guys are together again. Maybe someday I'll find someone. Kind of gives me hope . . ."

"If you want to find your perfect mate, I could teach you how to connect with your spirit guides."

"That's okay. I think for now I'll just connect with a pillow and blanket." He yawned. "Yeah, I never thought I'd live to see the day that I was the only celibate one left in the house."

* * *

The day went by way too quickly. Michael took Rose shopping, lavishing her with new toys and clothes. Next, he took her to a park, where she couldn't seem to get enough of being pushed on the swing. Gloria had packed a lunch, and they had a picnic together. Unfortunately, Rose's favorite sandwich was peanut butter. For her, he endured it.

By afternoon, the paparazzi had spied them and began snapping pictures and trailing them everywhere they went. At first, he tried to be nice and hoped that would appease them. But after a while, they were annoying guests that had overstayed their welcome. Rather than pitch a scene, he chose to take Rose home.

Gloria met them at the door. Pointing to the cameras aimed their way, she was glad for the gates that kept them some distance away. "I see you brought the zombies with you."

"I'm sorry. We tried to ditch them, didn't we, Rose?"

"Whatever. Come in. Hey, sweet girl, did you have a nice day with daddy?"

Rose could now speak in short sentences. "Daddy's fun. We ate peanut butter."

"Which Mommy knows I hate."

"Oh dear. Mommy forgot." Gloria scooped Rose from Michael's arms. "Would daddy like an adult beverage and to stay for dinner?" Gloria smiled at him. "Then daddy can tuck you in bed for the night. I'm sure you're a tired girl." She turned to Michael. "I made your favorite dish, just in case."

"Did you score some ricin, Gloria?"

"Stop it, Michael. I've been thinking about what you said. You're right. We need to put Rose first."

"When you're nice, I get confused. What do you really want?"

"Honestly. I don't want a thing from you." The nanny came in, and Gloria handed Rose off. "Please, Felicia, give her a bath, and then she can join us for dinner before bedtime." She turned back to Michael. "Come on. Help me make the salad."

Michael nodded to Felicia, following Gloria into the kitchen. Pulling a long knife from the butcher block, she was still smiling. "Can you chop up some vegetables?"

"I'm having flashbacks to one of those forensic shows."

Gloria laughed. "There was actually a time when we liked each other. I forget. What changed that?"

"Does it really matter anymore?" Gingerly, he took the knife from her as if it was a murder weapon, and he didn't want to leave incriminating fingerprints. "I think you hated me first."

"Hate is such a strong word. Two sides of the coin, love and hate. By the way, you look great. I see you're still sticking with the virus story."

"Why wouldn't I? It's true, and I'm fine. Despite your dour predictions, I made it through the tour. But you caused quite a frenzy. You really know how to steal the show without even being present. Thanks to you, I had to answer to that one. As you can imagine, your name was synonymous with bitch."

"Speaking of, I heard about that love ballad to the girl from Marysville. Hearts were broken around the world."

"Don't start with her, or we will finish this conversation right now."

"Ah, how sweet. You're fucking her. Which, quite frankly, I wasn't sure you were capable of after surgery and chemotherapy."

Michael was still. "I have no idea what you're talking about." He had stopped chopping.

"Really? I think you do. Here's the thing, Michael, what's it worth to you for me to keep your secret?"

Michael swallowed. "Wherever you're getting your information, you're misinformed."

"Let's just say I have a reliable source." She smiled. "It's too late, Michael. Stay away from Rose. I'm not going to let you humiliate me again. Stay away or I'll tell the whole world your secret." She was solemn. "You know, I always thought it'd feel good to hurt you. But you know what? You make me feel like I just slapped a child."

Michael sat quietly, studying her before finally speaking. "If you think you can pull this off without my taking action, you are foolish. I'm not afraid to tell people I have cancer. I can tweet it right now. Actually, I'll do one better. I'll tell them you won't let me see my daughter because I'm sick. That ought to get their attention. What kind of a bitch would do that? I can't imagine the hate mail you'll be getting after that."

Rose burst into the room, her tiny arms outstretched. "Daddy!"

He put his arms around her, pulling her onto his lap. "I love you, baby girl." He turned to Gloria. "Before I go home, I'll be meeting with my attorney to file for full custody. Before this is over, you will deeply regret your attempt to manipulate me."

When she didn't answer him, he patted Rose on her fluffy head. "I have to go. See you soon." He shot a glance over to Gloria. "If you feel guilty it's because, in fact, you did just slap a child. This would do nothing to me, but would certainly hurt Rose. And you know, I remember now why I didn't like you anymore. I got it this time, Gloria. I never forget."

Chapter 52

The first thing Michael did was consult his attorney to make sure everything was legal. The second thing he did was call the nanny. Lastly, he made sure everything was ready to for Rose's transition to his home. When he showed up on Gloria's doorstep with two police officers, there was nothing she could do.

Gloria was stunned. "You cannot simply walk in here and take Rose."

The police officer intervened. "You have a shared parenting agreement. He has full rights to her. I'm sorry."

Gloria was stammering. "But I didn't marry Nick! I honored your request. How can you justify this?" She was sobbing.

"You only postponed the wedding. I think I made myself clear. Rose is going to spend the summer in Maui. You always get to have her. Why should I only have visitation rights? It's very important to me to have a relationship with my daughter. So she's coming to Maui. I love her, too."

"But when is she coming home?" Gloria looked close to having a panic attack.

"We can discuss that later. Right now, she's going on summer vacation with me. If you want to come to Maui to visit with her, you know how to reach me."

"But Michael . . ."

Michael simply walked past her and gathered Rose in his arms. Felicia was putting everything into the limo that Michael had rented. Rose waved at her mommy. "Bye-bye, Mommy!"

Gloria was hysterical. "Please, Michael, you don't know her routines, you know nothing about her. She will cry for me."

"Felicia knows her routines. If I have any questions or concerns, I'll call you. I'm not trying to torture her. For god's sake, I just want to be able to spend time with her. If she is really miserable, I'll bring her home to you." Michael smiled. "Rose, give mommy a kiss."

Rose put out her arms. "Maui, Mommy."

Gloria burst into tears and ran into the house, slamming the door behind her.

Michael turned to Felicia. "You can handle Rose, right?"

Felicia nodded. "Yes, sir."

He sighed. "Just call me Michael. Let's go. DJ is waiting at the airport for us."

* * *

Anni remembered it as the day that everything changed in Maui. Sera slept with Michael. Joe and Anni now shared a room. Felicia had a bedroom adjacent to Rose's room. DJ declared his room off limits. Since it was a six-bedroom bungalow, aka mansion, there was one guest room left. The entire energy in the house changed from formal to a huge playground.

It quickly became apparent that Michael adored Rose and loved being a father to her. Rose adapted quickly to her new environment, but Michael spent a lot of his time with her. Sera became a sort of aunt to her, as did Anni. Rose even called them Aunt Seerah and Aunt Nanni. Joe became Uncle Jojo. Evenings at the pool consisted of everyone swimming and playing with little Rose. The nanny was delegated to bath time and taking care of her when the adults had other business to attend. Otherwise, Michael was an attentive father to her.

When Anni looked back on their years in Maui, she realized those were the best of times. She saw a side of Michael that, otherwise, she would have never witnessed. Joe agreed with her. With Rose, he had amazing patience and gentleness. He was never annoyed with her thousand questions, and every night, he personally tucked her into bed.

There was one night when she got sick and vomited all over him. Instead of asking the nanny to tend to her, he cleaned her up and tucked her into bed next to him. Sera lay next to them and watched him comfort her. Michael read her stories until Rose fell asleep in her daddy's arms. When Michael fell asleep, Sera covered them both with a sheet and slept in the hammock.

Rose was entertainment. Even DJ, when he was there, played with her. He would do funny things like bring her outrageous outfits and say she should be part of the band. He taught her songs, and she would dance for them. Michael was teaching her how to play the keyboards, which she thought was immense fun. Sera painted her nails and did her hair up in a ponytail. Anni and Joe took her to the beach to look for treasures. Rose was clearly the center of their universe.

Gloria called several times a week. Michael usually deferred to the nanny. Rose talked to her mother and told her she was having fun. Gloria never came to Maui to see Rose. She did marry Nick that summer and went on a honeymoon. Michael called his attorney again. For now, Rose would be staying with her father.

* * *

Michael and Sera sat patiently in the oncologist's office. It had been one year since he went into remission and time for the annual checkup, which had included lab work, X-rays and another CT scan. It seemed to be taking Dr. Laura Bryson longer than usual. Finally, she spoke. "I've reviewed everything, and I have a few concerns I'd like to discuss with you."

"Like what?" Michael clutched Sera's hand. "Is it the lungs again? I haven't been coughing up blood."

"Have you been more fatigued lately? Any discomfort?"

Sera did a quick rewind.

She woke up in the night and reached for Michael, but he wasn't next to her. Tiptoeing to the bathroom, she saw him swallowing a handful of pills. "Are you okay?"

"I think I have the flu. I ache all over."

"Come back to bed. I'll massage your back with eucalyptus oil."

"That's okay. I think I'll sleep in the hammock. You go ahead and get your rest. I am so exhausted, but can't seem to sleep."

She also noticed he had lost weight. "Can I get you something to eat?"

"I'm not hungry."

"You haven't eaten all day."

"I'll have some more tea."

"You can't live on tea, Michael."

"I'll eat something after I wake up."

Sera realized Dr. Bryson was still speaking. "There are some spots on your liver and a lesion at the base of your spine. I'd like to try another round of chemotherapy and start some more radiation therapy."

Michael closed his eyes. "This cannot be happening. What happened to the remission part?"

"I'm sorry." Dr. Bryson actually looked sad. "I'd like to admit you to the hospital for the first round. You have a history of severe reactions, and these drugs are not without serious complications."

Sera found her voice, but it sounded far away. "What kind of complications?"

"We're talking renal failure, which is a shutdown of the kidneys or total destruction of your immune system. I want you under close medical supervision."

Michael asked. "What about experimental drugs? Clinical trials? What other choices do I have?"

Dr. Bryson nodded. "Of course, we can explore all of those options. But for now, we need to start with chemo and radiation again."

Michael nodded. "What are my chances?"

"You beat it once. Stay positive. We'll do absolutely everything we can. So can we get started next week?"

"What about medical marijuana?"

Dr. Bryson nodded. "If you want to try it, I can order it for you."

"Yeah." Michael nodded back. "At this point, I'll try anything."

* * *

It was the perfect way to end the day. Anni and Joe were relaxing quietly by the pool, sipping wine, when Sera came out and sat down beside them. She rarely drank, so when she poured about a half a bottle of wine into a glass, they knew something was wrong.

"What's the matter?" Anni protectively put her arm around her.

"It's Michael. He didn't want to tell anyone, but we went for his annual exam today."

Joe sat down his glass. "What is it?"

Her voice was soft. "There are spots on his liver and a lesion on his spine. That means more chemo and radiation."

"Oh no." Anni looked to Joe.

Sera murmured. "Lately, he's been tired and said he thought he had the flu. It never occurred to me it could be something more."

Anni hugged her. "We'll get through this together. We did it before, we'll do it again."

Joe rallied. "We'll fight this together. Team Dolanski."

Sera smiled weakly. "Thanks. I'm never been so afraid in my life."

Anni tried to sound optimistic. "He's strong, remember?"

"I can't lose him." Sera looked scared. "I love him."

"Don't give up, Sera. Michael is a fighter," said Joe. But even as he said that, he felt afraid.

Chapter 53

If yesterday hadn't driven home the facts, the following week did. Michael checked into the hospital. Radiology came by and changed his lower spine into a roadmap with a red marker. He wondered if he would glow in the dark. *Glow in the dark pop stars. Collect them all . . .*

Sera sat next to him while they started an intravenous solution containing the magic elixir which was supposed to attack the cancer cells. Michael watched the tiny droplets of fluid plop into the chamber above his head. Threading their way down the plastic tube, the drops entered his veins and mixed with his blood. He imagined they were traveling around inside his body gobbling up diseased cells like little PAC-MANs.

Michael refused to allow them to call Gina, stating, "Let's not worry her. When I was a kid and got sick, she ended up puking beside me. She'll just freak out, and I don't need that right now."

Joe agreed. *He didn't need it, either.*

Sera practically carried him into the house. Michael had no more than reached the door when he got sick. There was nothing simple about his reaction to chemotherapy. Joe relieved Sera for a few hours so she could rest before a long night. Michael lay across his bed, clutching a beach towel and an emesis basin from the hospital. Joe's job consisted of wiping his forehead with a cool cloth and attempting to distract him whenever possible.

"I know it's hard for you," Joe stroked Michael's hair away from his face with the damp cloth. "I'm so sorry you have to go through this again. How much longer will you need to continue with treatments?"

"I don't know. I guess until it cures me or kills me. Right now, I'd rather die from cancer than puke myself to death."

Joe turned to Anni, who had just come into Michael's bedroom. "Does anything help him?"

"I have an injection for nausea. If this works, we're in business, and he can sleep for a while."

"This is cruel." Joe murmured. "I couldn't stand it."

"I know," Anni eased Michael onto his side. "Just a tiny prick in your left hip."

"You're good. I didn't even feel it, or I'm just numb now."

She pulled the blankets over him. "Try to rest. You should feel the effects in about fifteen minutes."

He nodded, too sick to speak anymore. Ten minutes later, he was dozing. Joe turned to Anni. "If I'm ever this sick, I'll forego chemotherapy. There is no dignity in vomiting yourself to death."

* * *

Someone always managed to bring Rose in to see her father every day. They tried to arrange it so that he wasn't sleeping or sick. Even though the visits were usually short, it seemed to cheer Michael up to see her little face and listen to her chatter. As for Rose, she seemed to sense her daddy was sick. She'd come toddling in with her doctor kit and put her toy stethoscope on him, pretending to listen to his heart, though, apparently Rose must have thought his heart moved around, as she sometimes, put it on his arm or stomach. "Hurt, Daddy, get well." She would touch him in various places: his eyes, ears, nose, mouth, and ask, "Ouch?"

Michael played along. "No, that doesn't hurt." She would try again to figure out what hurt. Finally, she put her tiny hand on his chest. "That hurts." He smiled at her. "All better now. Thank you, Rose." Satisfied she had found the part that was broken and had fixed it, she would give him a kiss, then hop down. "Welcome, Daddy."

*   *   *

Michael could hear DJ laughing on his cell phone somewhere down the hall. Peering at the clock on his nightstand, he realized it was only seven o'clock in the evening. He couldn't recall falling asleep. Lately, the days and nights had blended together. It was no wonder that DJ was seldom at home. There was nothing fun going on around here, unless you enjoyed watching someone sleep or puke.

Moving in slow motion, he hauled himself off the bed. It wasn't that he felt particularly sick, rather drained and empty. Wincing at his reflection in the mirror, he turned on the shower. The hot waterfall eased the aching in his lower back and legs. Leaning against the wall, he closed his eyes. Later, if he could drag himself to the lanai, he'd hit the Jacuzzi for a while. For the first time ever, he was grateful for being a visionary and installed an elevator.

"Are you okay?" DJ rapped on the door.

"Yeah, I'm fine."

"I'm going out for a while, if that's good with you?"

"You don't need my permission."

"I won't be late."

"Yes, you will. Have some fun for both of us."

He heard DJ mumble something as the door softly closed.

Michael slowly slid down the wall, dissolving into a puddle on the floor. He wasn't sure how long he was lying there, but it finally occurred to him that he needed to turn off the water or drown. Pulling himself to his feet, he wrapped himself in a towel and made it back to the bed. Collapsing, he decided the Jacuzzi would have to wait. He picked up the remote, punched the button and curtains circled his bed, enclosing him in a shroud of privacy.

*   *   *

Chapter 54

That's how Sera found him. Asleep, naked and wet. Carefully, she pulled the towel away and covered him with a blanket and lay down next to him. Sometimes she just listened to him breathe. Lightly, she caressed his forehead, gently playing with his hair.

To her surprise, he rolled over, smiling at her, "Hey, you."

"Hey." Smiling back, she added, "Did you try to drown yourself?"

"Almost." Touching her face, he added, "But I wasn't successful. Why don't we try the Jacuzzi? I might have better luck there."

She helped him into a robe, and they slowly made their way, pausing a few times so he could steady himself.

"I feel so weak and dizzy."

"You'll be stronger once the treatments are done." She had her arm around him and could feel him trembling. "Maybe the Jacuzzi isn't a good idea."

Sera joined him in the bubbling hot water.

"Oh my god, this feels so good." He sighed. "Look at all those stars tonight. Oh look, a shooting star." Pointing to the heavens, he said, "There's another one. Did you see it, Sera?"

She nodded. "You're supposed to make a wish."

"I wish for a cure, and whether it comes in an oil or an IV, I really don't care. What is your wish?"

"Marry me." She cupped his face in her hands, turning him toward her. "Marry me, Michael."

He looked away. "Oh, Sera, isn't it enough that we're together? You know that I love you."

"But I want everyone to know that we have a commitment to each other."

"I am committed to you. We don't need a piece of paper." He paused. "Do we?"

"I lost you once. I don't want to lose you again."

Michael put his arm around her. "I won't do that to you ever again." He pulled her closer. "But, Sera, I can't promise that I won't leave you. I don't want to die, and if you have a cure, sign me up. This time, if I leave you, it won't be because I want to go. Do you understand what I'm saying to you?"

She stopped him. "Don't talk like that. You're going to get through this. I have to believe that."

"Believe me, I pray you're right. But what I'm trying to tell you is that we don't need some symbolic piece of paper. I'll take care of you. You have my word."

Chapter 55

Since it was Sunday morning, Michael knew exactly where to find Joe. Since he didn't own a car, he borrowed DJ's Lamborghini and drove to Our Lady Queen of Angels Catholic Church. Sitting quietly in the last pew, he watched the priest go through the rituals of mass. He watched as everyone kneeled in prayer, making an invisible cross motion at certain intervals. Communion came next, which was the part where a sip of wine and something that looked like a piece of tissue paper mysteriously became holy elements.

As Joe turned to go sit back down after communion, he saw Michael sitting in the back of the church. After mass was over, he walked back and sat down next to him. "What brings you here? I have a hunch it isn't because you got up this morning and decided to become Catholic."

Michael laughed softly, "Because I knew where I'd find you. Incidentally, what does it take to be a priest? I mean, did you go to priest school or something?"

Joe smiled. "If you're considering the priesthood, I must warn you, you won't like the music, and the pay sucks."

"Father Dolanski? You know, that actually sounds like a good name for a band." He was still smiling. "Probably already taken. Oh well. Why do you cross yourself? What's does that mean?"

"Well, okay, though I'm not sure why you are playing twenty catechism questions, however, as an expression of personal devotion, Christians bless themselves to signify their love and devotion to Christ. According to St. Ambrose, the sign of the cross is on your brow to help us remember Christ, on our hearts so we may always love him, and on our shoulders so we always carry out his work. Whenever the priest blesses or absolves the congregation he traces a cross in the air with his uplifted hand. That's what you saw today, it is symbolic."

"Symbolic. Like a piece of paper for marriage?"

"You know, for about a minute, I thought I knew where this might be going, but I have to confess, I'm lost."

Michael leaned back. "She wants to marry me. Isn't that the most absurd thing you've ever heard?"

Joe watched the flickering votive candles near the altar. Every candle lit was a silent prayer for a loved one or as a tribute to someone they had lost. "In the church, marriage is a holy sacrament. It's an outward sign of an inward and visible grace."

"I'm sorry. You're losing me. I just need a simple answer."

"Okay. Here it is. It's important to her. What else do you need?"

Chapter 56

Two days later, Michael sat with Sera on the verge of dawn at Haleakala volcano, waiting for the sunrise above the clouds. It was cool, but not cold, and they both had on sweaters. As the sunrise crested, Michael turned to her. "There will never be anyone in my life that I love as much as you. You ask for nothing, and yet I want to give you everything. You are my friend, my guide, and the love of my life." He slipped something comparable to the Hope diamond onto her finger, though it was edged in turquoise to symbolize her heritage. "Sera, I'm honored to accept your marriage proposal. I only want to be worthy of that honor. I am humbled by your devotion to me."

The only thing Sera could do was cry. "I've never known anyone like you. You are my very best friend and the love of my life. I know you are giving me this gift, and I am also humbled by your devotion to me. I am beyond honored to be your wife."

* * *

It was a simple ceremony on the beach. Sera wore a white sundress and carried wild flowers she had handpicked on Maui. Michael was dressed in a suave soft grey Armani, his dark hair blowing in his face. They were married by a justice of the peace and recited an Apache wedding vow. Anni played bridesmaid while Joe watched from the sidelines. DJ was best man, and Gina cried. Rose was the little flower girl. It took less than ten minutes. When the ceremony was over, Sera gave Anni her bouquet. "I hope these bring you good luck." Anni hugged her, and both women held each other, crying with joy.

Michael nudged Joe. "Why are they crying?"

"They're happy."

"I don't get it."

Joe smiled. "I think it's a girl thing."

Michael nodded in agreement. "Yeah. I've never seen a guy bubble up over a wedding."

Afterward, they had dinner at home prepared by their personal chef. Gina stayed overnight, and everyone spent the evening relaxing by the pool. Since Gina hadn't seen Rose since she was an infant, it was a reunion for her and Rose. Gina seemed a little awkward with her, as if she wasn't quite sure what to do with her.

The next day, as a wedding gift, DJ personally flew them to Aspen, Colorado, where his father owned a log cabin for vacationing. DJ said it best, "When you live in paradise, where can you go from here?"

Before Michael left, he handed an envelope to DJ. "Next week, I want you to post this press release. It's our wedding announcement and also addresses my health. No one needs to know what kind of cancer. I'll set up some interviews when I return."

Chapter 57

Sera had never imagined how wonderful two weeks could be in the splendor of the Colorado Rockies. She loved the snow-capped mountains, cool blue skies, and shimmering aspens. She and Michael went for long walks and breathed in the crisp mountain air. In the evening, they curled up in front of a roaring fireplace while Michael played his guitar, often talking until dawn.

They made a pact of never talking about cancer. There were no televisions or newspapers. They had no idea what impact Michael's marriage announcement had on the rest of the world. Sera was just happy that everyone knew that she was Mrs. Dolanski. That was enough for now.

But sometimes, in the night, lying next to her husband, she heard him moaning softly. There were times when they went walking and he had to stop, and she felt a cold chill that had nothing to do with the mountain air. When they finished making love, she noticed her husband cried out. It had never dawned on her until now that his tears were not the result of ecstasy, but that he was in pain. Once again, she felt like the little girl running into the dark night. *Please, show me what to do.*

* * *

Reporters swarmed DJ the instant he set foot in Dallas. Cursing Michael under his breath, he threw up his arms, trying to push the paparazzi away.

"Is Michael dying? What kind of cancer? Is that why he married his high school sweetheart? What is his prognosis? Who is Seraphine Rosewood? Is he getting chemotherapy? What's going to happen to you and the band?"

"I wish I knew." DJ thundered. "I don't have any answers."

"Where is Michael right now?"

He was seriously tempted to tell them.

"Has he left the country in search of a cure?" someone shouted.

"He's on his honeymoon and in search of peace and relaxation, which is more than I'll get." DJ snarled. "Now, leave me alone. I don't have any answers. You can ask him."

* * *

Michael and Sera had been home for about a week. Rose was delighted to have her father back home, and he seemed just as happy to be with her again. But after a few days, he had to go back to work. The band had assembled in their Honolulu studio, so Michael and DJ left. It was back to work.

Officially, Sera was now Rose's stepmother, which was a new role for her. Actually, she didn't feel it really changed anything. Rose still called her Aunt Seerah, which was fine with her. Titles could complicate things, and Gloria was still her mother. With Michael gone, she decided to spend more time with Rose. It was the first time in her life she ever played mother to a child. Due to Michael's medical status, she was fully aware they would never have children together, so this would be as close to motherhood as she ever ventured. For now, she would enjoy the time as much as she could.

* * *

"I want to do this song over again. It's not right. It's supposed to be a love song. You're playing it too fast. DJ, soft and easy, like you're making love to her not beating her up. Just play it gently, okay?"

DJ bit his lip to keep from snapping. All day long, the entire band had been trying to please him. But Michael had been giving orders like a marine. Speed up this part. No, now slower. Play it louder. Now do it softer. You're coming in on this verse too early. Don't be late this time. Sing it an octave higher. Now lower. That's worse. Make it better next time. It was enough to drive everyone into a schizophrenic frenzy.

"I give up. I'm going home." DJ threw down his drumsticks. "Not that there is any peace there either. Not since you moved in a priest, a nurse, and a wife. You sure know how to cover all the angles, Michael."

Michael gave him a sharp glance. "I consider them to be my family. If you don't want to play, go home. I'll figure out what to do without you. What's wrong with you today? Why can't you just play this song for me?"

DJ glared at him. "It's just like you to act cute now. Let's just finish the set so we can all go home. That is, if I still have a room there. You didn't move in anyone else today, did you?"

Michael toyed with the strings on his guitar. "This is probably our last recording. I just want it to be perfect." He inspected the group solemnly. "So let's get it right this time. Shall we?"

* * *

Michael hopped into the passenger seat of DJ's lambo. "I'm quitting, DJ."

"Quitting what?" DJ looked confused

Michael sighed. "The band. I can't do this anymore."

DJ turned to him. "Say what?"

"This is not easy for me, but I'm leaving. I'm sorry, DJ."

"That's just great news, Michael." DJ stomped on the accelerator. "Perfect end to a shitty day."

* * *

Joe knew there was trouble the moment DJ and Michael burst through the door and stomped into the house. DJ went to one side of the room, and Michael went the other way, like two kids after a fight on the playground.

DJ started. "Why do you want to ruin a good thing? We make great music together. We need your leadership. Without you, we're just another band."

"I've got too much on my mind, DJ. I can't concentrate on music anymore."

"So what are we supposed to do without you?"

"I don't know. You'll figure it out."

"What if I don't want to figure it out, Michael? What are you trying to tell me?"

"I'm telling you that you don't need me." Michael flopped into a chair as DJ paced around the room.

"I can understand if you want to take a sabbatical. I get that. Take some time. But don't leave us. We need you."

"DJ, I can't. I'm sorry."

"Damn you, Michael. I'm the one that gets all the dirty work. I got the privilege of being asked a hundred questions I can't answer. Lately, it's been pretty tough being your friend. I don't want to think about a future without you." DJ fell into the nearest chair, hands over his face. Joe had never seen him like this. "I'm sorry. I've been trying, but I don't know what to say or do anymore, Michael."

"What do you expect from me, DJ? I'm going to fight as hard as I can. But I'm tired. What little energy I have left, I need for that fight."

"I can't go on without you, buddy." DJ looked close to tears. "You're gonna beat this, right? Is that right, Michael?"

Michael looked sad. "I'm really trying, DJ. But I'm not sure anymore."

Chapter 58

It was past midnight when Joe heard someone playing the keyboards and tiptoed down the hall. It was dark, only moonlight bathed the room in an ethereal glow, casting ghostly shadows. Joe decided to stay out of sight and not disturb him. He stood quietly, hidden in the shadows, watching as Michael's fingers nimbly caressed the keys with the perfection of Mozart. He moved gracefully up and down the keyboard, going faster and harder, cresting and falling, never missing a single note.

At the end of the song, he began to play the same chaotic melody over again. Effortlessly striking the dancing keys, he played at a manic pace. Without warning, he suddenly stopped and smashed both fists onto the keyboard. The clashing notes caused Joe to jump.

"I can't lose all this. I can't. I've worked too hard." Michael laid his head on the keyboard, breathing deeply, pounding his fists, over and over again, he started to make a whimpering sound, as if he were trying not to cry.

"This isn't fair. Not fair . . ." After a few minutes, he was quiet, and for a moment, Joe thought he had fallen asleep. Suddenly, he sat up, composed himself and began playing the Pachebel Canon. Silently, Joe went back to his room.

Chapter 59

"**If you come through this kitchen** one more time, I'm gonna scream." Anni shut the oven door, both hands on her hips.

"You'll ruin the soufflé." Michael grabbed a potholder off the counter and opened the oven door. "Ah, it's too late. How could you do this, Anni? It looks like a baked pancake."

"You opened the door a dozen times. It never had a chance for life," Anni snapped back, as he clicked off the oven and handed her the potholders.

"I guess we'll have to forget it and fix something else for breakfast." He stood staring at the ruined soufflé. "Maybe someone would like this, but I can't even bear to look at it anymore."

"I'd be delighted to fix something else Michael, but I can't even find the toaster."

"You want money to go shopping?" Michael hesitated. "We used to have a toaster. Where did it go, Anni?"

"Damned if I know." Anni smiled. "I don't want your money, Michael. Are you okay?"

"Sera went for a walk this morning without me. I don't know what I did wrong." He looked genuinely upset.

"This is really hard on all of us." Anni tucked a lock of hair behind her ear. "Give her some time."

"It doesn't matter. I'm stressing everyone out. I'm the one that ought to leave."

She watched him frantically gathering eggs out of the refrigerator, cracking them into a bowl. "What are you doing?"

"I'm making another soufflé."

"You want some help?"

"No, I want to ruin it myself."

"What is the matter with men? They can be so stubborn and linear in their thinking."

"What are you rambling about?" He was busily beating the eggs into a neurotic lather. "Hand me the cheese, will you?"

Anni marched out of the kitchen, but not before she heard him mutter.

"I should have invested in a Midol factory."

* * *

Sera was strolling along the beach, when she looked up and saw someone walking deliberately toward her. Instinctively, she knew it was Michael, even though the person was far away because she knew the way he walked. Even though he wasn't particularly tall, he carried himself in a way that made him seem taller and confident. Patiently, she waited for him. When he finally caught up with her, he took her hand, and without saying anything, led her to a quiet place where they sat down.

Michael stared out at the ocean. "I don't have to explain to you what's at stake here. I know you're a strong person, and that is just one of the many reasons I respect you. That said, I know this is overwhelming for all of us. When you are feeling that way, come to me so we can talk. Let me feel like I'm helping you, too."

Sera nodded. "The conversation between you and DJ was hard to take."

"I know. DJ isn't coping very well. We have to help him."

"I'm not sure if he will let me, Michael."

"It's probably my job, not yours. I've known him a long time, Sera. For the most part, he keeps his emotions tightly reigned in, then he just sort of bubbles over and it takes everyone by surprise. He took you by surprise. I'm not sure if this makes it any better or not, but he will shut down again."

She smiled at him. "I just needed to walk away for a while. Sometimes I have to get off by myself so I can think."

Michael smiled back at her, nodding. "Actually, let's take a ten-minute meditation so we can center ourselves and get rid of all this negativity. Afterward, I think we'll both feel better. I'll even take the lead. You can follow me."

She kissed him. "You know I'd follow you anywhere."

"I know. Now, instead of holding hands this time, put your arms around me."

"Okay." She laughed.

"I'm going to put my arms around you. Come closer." He smiled. "Just a little more."

She was pressed against him. With a chuckle, he gently eased her down to the sand. Slowly and seductively slipping his hand down along her breast, then he moved further down between her legs. She felt his fingers gently massaging her, until she couldn't stand it another minute. Arching her back, she pulled him toward her, wet with desire. They both laughed.

"I like your meditations, Michael."

"Ten minutes and I told you that we'd both be feeling better." Michael was back to his playful side. "Enough talk. Let's stay focused."

Afterward, Sera decided it was one of the best meditations she had ever experienced.

Chapter 60

After six months, Michael suddenly packed up little Rose and took her back to Gloria. At the time, no one understood, as they figured Rose would be staying indefinitely. Michael shook his head. "She needs to go back Gloria now." That was the only explanation he gave. Sera looked sad to see the little girl go away.

Sera offered to go with him, but he declined. "I need to do this alone."

When Michael returned from Malibu, he went to his room and didn't come out. The house seemed too quiet that night.

* * *

A few weeks later, Michael approached Joe. "Can you do me a favor?"

"Sure. What can I do, Michael?"

"I really hate to ask you, but could you go talk to Gloria. I want to see Rose."

"What did you say?" Joe leaned forward. "Why don't you go talk to her yourself?"

"I just want to see my daughter." Michael was pacing. "I'm sure Gloria threw a party after finding out I lost this battle."

"What battle?" Joe was confused.

Michael handed him a letter. "Rose went home because I lost custody of her. I was denied custody due to my medical condition.

That's why she went back to Gloria." Michael looked close to tears. "I miss her, Joe."

Joe shook his head. "I have to say, meeting with Gloria is about as cheery as standing in the middle of a freeway during rush hour and trying to avoid a head-on collision."

"But will you try?"

"I'll see what I can do."

"I'm grateful you'll try. Thank you, Joe."

"Don't thank me yet."

* * *

Joe was surprised when Gloria agreed to meet him.

"Father di Blasio. I assume you are here on Michael's behalf."

"I am."

"So what is your role? Is Michael trying to buy his way into heaven?"

"Actually, Michael is doing well. But he wants to see his daughter."

She laughed. "He's not fine, Michael is pissed off that he didn't win custody. So are you the new middle man? Did DJ get tired of playing the role?"

Rose toddled into the room. She was still a tiny ball of energy and adorable. "Hola, Jojo."

Joe smiled. "Hola, Miss Rose." She crawled onto his lap. "He misses her. Please Gloria. If you could find it in your heart . . ."

"If daddy dear is too sick to come by, he's too sick to play with Rose."

"What would it take to change your mind?"

"The only thing that matters to Michael is money, music, and manipulating people. Just to set the record straight. I know I'm not perfect, but he isn't going to ruin my life again. He just stole six months away from me, and he isn't going to get that opportunity one more time. He's just using you. You're nothing more than his ticket to heaven, just in case he needs to play that card. When he gets bored with you, he'll send you packing like he did to me. Michael is nothing more than a charming sociopath."

"All right, Gloria, I've had enough." He rose from his chair, sitting Rose on the floor. "Whether or not you like Michael is unimportant. I don't even care what happened between the two of you. But I do know this. You've hurt each other long enough. It has to stop. Someday you will live to regret these decisions. I know Michael . . . apparently better than you. I beg you to reconsider. He isn't playing games. He's sick, Gloria. Someday you can explain that to your daughter. But why am I telling you? You don't give a damn, do you?"

Gloria laughed. "Oh, come on now, Father. If he were so damned sick, why would he bother to marry Pocahontas from Pruneville?"

"You'd never understand." He didn't wait for a reply.

Chapter 61

Sleep was impossible for Sera. Michael kept thrashing wildly in his sleep, mumbling incoherently." *No. Get off me. Get away. No . . .*" Without warning, he screamed.

Joe and Anni were at the peak of lovemaking when they heard what sounded like a scene from *Psycho*. The both froze. Grabbing their robes, they ran downstairs.

DJ hit the floor at a dead run. Having only gotten home moments before, he'd just turned out the lights. His first thought was that someone had broken into the house.

Everyone converged at the same time. DJ turned on the light.

"Who screamed?" Joe was breathless. "Is everyone all right?"

Michael tried to laugh. "I had a bad dream. Go back to bed. I'm sorry."

Everyone stared at the bed, and Michael followed their gaze. He was covered in blood, which seemed to be coming from his nose and mouth. "Oh, fuck." His eyes were wide. "Now what?"

* * *

Michael was readmitted to the hospital. He was having extreme side effects to the chemotherapy. Sera took control of researching all options: clinical trial studies, immunotherapy, Machu Picchu, anything. Actually, it was Sera's suggestion to call Gina. Gina arrived, and suddenly they were best friends. Together, they began making calls, compared notes, and presented everything to Michael for his consideration.

Dr. Bryson put it simply. "It's not just that his white count is low, but that his entire immune system has been essentially compromised by all the radiation and chemotherapy. Quite frankly, at this point, he doesn't qualify for a clinical trial. If we can build him back up, interventional therapies may be an option. Radiofrequency ablation could be beneficial."

"What am I supposed to do now?" Michael asked.

"We're going to initiate treatments to build you back up. We'll start with some blood transfusions. We're going to have to place you in isolation until you're stronger. One germ could kill you."

Anni squeezed his hand. "I knew you were really a vampire."

Michael tried to smile. "Better than being a ghost, I guess."

"Hey." Joe held up a paper bag. "I brought you a gift." He pulled out a pair of red sneakers. "It was as close as I could get to red slippers on short notice."

Michael laughed softly. "I can't wait to wear them out of here."

As it turns out, that took another month.

Chapter 62

Three months later...

"*Mirror, mirror on the wall... who looks sicker after all.*"

Rinsing her mouth with cold water, Anni spit into the toilet and flushed away the vomit. It had been years since she had been honestly sick. With trembling hands, she reached for a washcloth and held it under cold water. Washing her face made her feel a little better. Ambling back to bed, she curled up in a tiny ball, wrapping herself in a down quilt.

Thank God, Michael and Sera were in California getting his final round of therapy. Last month, he had completed the ablation procedure on his spine. Everyone knew this was his final chance for a cure. They were all hanging onto a fragile sliver of hope. Michael had made it clear that if this didn't work, he wasn't going to keep putting himself through more treatments.

* * *

Anni closed her eyes. Sometimes it seemed incredible to her that almost two years ago, she had lived an ordinary life in a small northern town in California and worked as a nurse in a hospital. Then, Michael Dolanski flew into town, and she was transformed into a private caregiver to a celebrity, lived in paradise, and slept almost nightly with a priest. Her stomach was twisting into a tight ball again. "Where in the hell will I be two years from now?" Leaping to her feet, she made it to the bathroom in the nick of time.

Back in bed, she heard a knock on the door. Rolling over, she pulled the covers over her head. Joe knocked again, "Anni?" She ignored him. "Are you in there, Anni?"

She sighed. "I think I have the flu. Leave me alone."

"Can I get anything for you?"

"Stay away so you don't get it. Michael will be home in a few days. We can't have the flu going through here. Someone needs to be well."

There was silence. Good. He was gone. Her stomach was rock and rolling again. This time, she just used a waste basket by the bed.

* * *

Michael and Sera arrived home from the hospital. Sera helped him into the house, as he was attempting to precariously balance himself on crutches. Michael was the color of rice cakes.

"I thought I looked bad, but you look awful, Anni." Michael observed her intently. "Are you okay?"

"I've been sick for a week. Just be glad you missed it, Michael."

"What's wrong?" It was Sera.

"The flu, I guess." Anni faked a smile. "On the bright side, I think I lost ten pounds."

Michael was watching her intently. "You know, ginger tea helps."

"I've tried ginger, but it didn't help much."

"Sera has me taking all this holistic stuff that's supposed to be a natural cure for cancer. Maybe she can recommend something for you."

"Yeah, well . . . thanks, but I'll be fine." Anni shrugged. "I'm glad you're both back home. It's been too quiet around here."

"I'd like to sit by the pool. I'm so sick of hospital rooms. I need fresh air and sunshine. That might help you, too."

Anni hugged them both. "Sure. Sounds good."

"Where's Joe?" asked Michael.

"I don't know." Anni answered him. "I'm sure he's close by."

Michael was quiet. He turned to Sera. "Would you mind getting us all some iced tea?"

Sera nodded. Turning to Anni, she added, "He's kind of wobbly on his crutches."

"I've got him." She took his arm, steadying him. "How long have you had these?"

"About two hours. I feel like a drunk trying to walk a straight line."

Anni laughed. "Which is exactly what you look like."

After settling into chaise lounges, Michael reached over, touching her arm. "Are you really okay, Anni?"

"Just fine." She sounded too optimistic. "Stop worrying about me. Don't you have enough on your mind?"

"Maybe you should see a doctor?" Michael sighed.

"Really, Michael, I am feeling better. It kind of comes and goes."

"What do you mean?"

"I feel better as the day progresses. Mornings are the worst. That, and I'm so tired all the time." Anni shrugged. "Anyway, I'm better today."

"Have you had a fever? Vomiting?"

"No, fever, but nausea and vomiting, yes." Anni wrinkled her nose at him. "What do you think Dr. Dolanski?"

Sera arrived with the tea. "Here you go. I made it fresh, with mint leaves."

Anni stared at the green leaves floating in the tea and felt a sudden wave of nausea. "If you'll excuse me . . ." She ran for the nearest bathroom.

Sera frowned. "What's the matter with her? I thought she was better?"

Michael spoke calmly. "I've seen this type of flu before. I don't think she's going to be better for a while."

Chapter 63

"So what's up, Joe?" Michael sauntered onto the lanai where Joe was seated and sort of toppled into a chair.

Joe was absorbed in reading a letter and jumped. "Oh my gosh, Michael! When did you get home? It's so good to see you." He frowned. "Why are you on crutches?"

"Radiation tends to chew holes in your bones. Just another delightful side effect from radiation. As you know, I've been in isolation the entire time which is why I told you and Anni to stay home. You didn't miss anything. It's really not been any fun at all, and I won't do it again. Though, I will say, the nausea has subsided, thanks to medical marijuana. So now I'm hooked on painkillers and pot." He smiled. "But see how happy I am?"

Joe laughed. "Can you share? I think Anni needs a hit."

"What's wrong with Anni?"

"She's had the flu."

"Have you bothered to take her to a doctor?"

"No . . . I mean, she's a nurse. If she thought she needed to see someone . . ."

Michael patted him on the shoulder. "It's not like Anni to be sick. Maybe a checkup would be a good idea."

"Okay." Joe nodded. "By the way, I got this letter today in the mail." He handed it to Michael.

Michael scanned the letter and looked over at Joe. "So it's official. You're no longer Father di Blasio?"

Joe smiled. "I plan to take Anni to dinner and ask her tomorrow night."

"Maybe I'm now the one being obtuse, but what are you asking her tomorrow night?"

"After all this time, she may not want me. But I'm going to ask her to marry me."

Despite illness, Michael's eyes were always full of life. "I think you have good timing on this one. I have a hunch she'll say yes." He tilted his head as if in thought. "You did get her a ring, right?"

Joe paused. "Oh god. Where do I get one of those?"

Michael had a mischievous grin. "Be grateful I'm back to save you. We need to go buy something that would be meaningful to her. I'll help you. You can thank me later."

Joe nodded. "Thank you, Michael. This really isn't my area of expertise."

"What were you going to do? Give her a rosary?"

"I'm sorry, Michael. I've never done this before."

Michael let out a long sigh. "It's okay. I have you covered. Now, just try to create a romantic moment, okay? I can't do that for you." He winked at him.

Chapter 64

"**Would you like** a glass of wine?"

"No, thank you." Anni was wearing a loose-fitting cashmere sweater and comfortable capris.

"I've never known you to turn down a glass of wine." Smiling, he reached across the table, gently touching her hand. "I know you've been sick, but you look beautiful tonight."

"Thank you."

"Two-word sentence game?"

"I guess."

"Are you hungry?"

"Not really."

"Then let's get out of here. How about a walk on beach? It's almost a full moon."

"Sounds nice."

"Let's go."

Shimmers of pale moonlight danced like sparkling fairies across the still waters as if they had been freed from the deepest and darkest depths of the ocean. For a long time, they walked in silence with the warm tide intermittently washing over their feet.

"Anni . . ." Taking both of her hands, he pulled her toward him. The moon cast a soft glow across her face. The wind was as soft as the moonlight. Tonight, she was Selene, the goddess of the moon. He placed the ring in her hand, "If you need some time to think about it, I'll understand. It's my turn to be patient. As of yesterday, I'm no longer a priest. I wanted to wait until I got an official notice. But if you would, I mean, will you even consider marrying me?"

"Shut up." Her face crumbled as she held the ring in her hand. "It's beautiful, Joe." It was a diamond edged in rubies, her birthstone, and one sapphire for Joe's birthday.

"Can I take that as a yes?" Kissing her deeply, he remembered their first time on the beach, and hoped for an encore tonight.

"First, there's something I need to tell you."

"Of course, Anni. You can tell me anything."

"I'm pregnant, Joe."

* * *

"So did she say yes?" Michael had a confident smirk.

Joe smiled back. "What do you think?"

"I think you played close to the sun on that one."

"She's pregnant, Michael."

"No kidding?" Michael said sarcastically, but his eyes were sparkling. "Congratulations. Now you get to be a real father."

"The doctor said she's due in about seven months. I can't even begin to grasp the concept of being a father, but thanks for helping me out. She loved the ring." He took a deep breath. "I wish we had known each other a long time ago."

"You wouldn't have liked me." Michael sniffed.

"Why do you say that?"

"Because I wouldn't have liked you." Michael half-smiled. "But I like you now."

Finally, they both laughed.

"So when is the big day?"

"Anni is thinking about it. She doesn't want to get sick at the altar."

"I totally get that." Michael blushed. "At least do I get to be best guy?"

"Absolutely. Who else?" Joe paused. "You're my best friend. If it weren't for you, I wouldn't be where I am today. And I know in this day and age, it might sound hokey, but I love you."

"Is it because I'm so sexy?" Michael winked. "Yeah, I know what you mean. Love you, too, Joe."

Chapter 65

Two months later

Of course, they chose to be married in the church. Michael watched with keen interest. When the rings were exchanged, the priest made that little cross sign and said it was an outward and visible sign of an inward and spiritual grace. He also most spoke out loud, *"Ah, now I know where you got that line. Cheater."*

When he married Sera, the ceremony took less than fifteen minutes, and they were barefoot on the beach. This ordeal went on for forty minutes and mostly it seemed to be a litany of rituals older than Rome. Somewhere in the middle of it all, he guessed it was official because the priest blessed them and pronounced they were husband and wife. In the end, it was sealed with the traditional kiss. Good enough. Joe was now an honest man.

Chapter 66

Sera had pulled together all of Michael's medical records and sent them to one of those centers that specialized in terminal cancer cases.

"What did they say?"

Sera didn't want to tell him. "They declined to see you. They can't help you."

Michael looked stunned. "Okay. This is probably it, Sera."

Sera held him. "Let's keep looking. We can't give up."

Michael looked sad. "I'm not going through anymore, Sera. Believe me, I know when I've lost a fight."

* * *

When Joe was growing up, family bonding was centered around having dinner together. It was a tradition left over from a time when mothers mostly stayed at home and fathers brought home a paycheck. However, since Joe's father was seldom present, he never recalled any outstanding memorable moments, but he did like gathering together at the end of the day. In Maui, that seemed to be at sunset and poolside with a bottle of wine. Some of the chatter was light, and sometimes it was deeper. Tonight, it was Michael's turn to start the dialogue.

"So, Joe and Anni, where do you see yourselves, let's say two years from now?"

Anni answered first. "Maybe another child, I'm not sure, though. I definitely don't see myself going back into nursing."

Michael turned to Joe. "What say, Joseph?"

Joe smiled. "I've always thought I'd make a good counselor."

"Well," Michael had on his glasses, which always gave him a studious, all-business look. "Those are noble ventures, but neither of those things will make you rich."

Joe was halfway through a bottle of wine, while Anni floated on the wind in the hammock. Anni asked, "Where is this going, Michael?"

"I promised to take care of you, if you stayed here with me. I want to honor that promise."

Sera sat quietly, holding Michael's hand. To Anni, she looked like she was trying to remain composed, wondering where she might be in two years. Anni spoke. "No Michael, we'll figure it out. You need to stay focused on you."

"Okay," Michael sighed. "I'm not trying to be morbid here, but this is important to me. Please, let me do this for you. You have both done so much for me. So I've been talking with DJ's father. I have some ideas."

Anni started to object, but Joe cut her off. "I know what I want to do. I want to be a counselor to kids who, without my guidance, would never have a chance. Maybe I won't be rich, but I'll be content, knowing that something I did mattered."

Michael raised an eyebrow and looked quizzically at him. "Hmmm . . . okay, Joe, you don't look like a manager of a juice bar, anyway. What about you, Anni?"

"You know my heart, Michael."

"All right," Michael sighed. "Sera and I are leaving next week and will be in Dallas. I have several meetings set up and that includes meetings with my attorneys. DJ will be there. We'll figure out the details. Stay tuned for updates."

* * *

Michael and Sera stayed for a week in Dallas. Of course, Michael introduced Sera to DJ's family. If Michael's home was a mansion, this was place was a king's palace, complete with a full staff that waited on them, catering to every need. Sera felt like Cinderella.

The second thing Sera noticed was that DJ's parents obviously considered Michael to be their son. DJ's mother held Michael in her arms, and he accepted her display of affection, without any hesitation. Michael didn't push her away. If she asked him a question, he answered her directly. There was no question that they loved and respected each other. She had assumed DJ's father would be all business. Instead, he was warm and welcoming. The first thing he did was gave her a hug and told her that if Michael loved her, he loved her. Sera quickly came to realize why Michael seldom went back home. She also saw DJ in another light. He was like his parents, warm, generous, and protective of his little brother.

During that time, Sera enjoyed getting to know DJ's mother. She was the kind of person that if you could order the perfect mother from a catalog, this would be the one to pick. While Michael was behind closed doors with Mr. Jansen, they sat on the terrace sipping iced tea and visiting.

"Michael told me how you rescued him, Mrs. Jansen. I know he is grateful, but I want to tell you that I'm also thankful. I saw what Claire did to him."

"Please call me, Marilee." She had a warm smile. "Luckily, I am able to do more than some, because financially we can afford to help. My purpose was to give Michael a chance. But he had to do the work. He had to want to make a better life for himself."

"But I can tell that you love him. He loves you. You became his family."

She nodded. "At first, he was very guarded, but I understood where that was coming from. So I was patient with him. I knew he needed consistency in his life. Gradually, he began to trust us and drop his defenses. After that, he blossomed into a new person. What's not to love about Michael?"

Sera nodded in return. "I know he's meeting with your husband, his father, making arrangements and taking care of things before he can't anymore." She blinked back tears. "After all these years, we found each other again, and now I'm afraid I'm losing him."

Marilee had beautiful blue eyes that were rimmed with tears. "Michael thought we saved him, but really he was a gift to us. I learned how to be patient and help someone that was struggling with emotional pain. Going through that process with him and seeing the successful person he grew into, has given me immeasurable joy. I know he views you as the inspiration of his life, he told me that. Hold onto that thought. I know I will treasure the lessons and joys he has taught to me. No matter what happens next, I am grateful he came into our lives." They held onto each other and cried.

After spending a week in the glow of their warmth, she almost wanted to stay and not return to Maui. When Michael said goodbye, his parents held onto to him and cried. Sera couldn't help herself, and she cried, too.

* * *

Before, DJ flew them back home to Maui, his mother privately pulled him aside. "How are you, DJ?" She looked genuinely concerned, and he could see that she had been crying.

DJ shook his head. "I'm not even sure how to answer that anymore. It's been one helluva journey."

"You know your father and I are here, if you need anything. If there is anything we can do . . ."

DJ gave her a strong hug. "I know I don't tell you this enough, but you have always been wonderful. I'm grateful for parents like you."

* * *

Sera often thought about Marilee's words and wondered, what would be the circumstances when she met DJ's parents the next time? Before she left, Marilee gave her a package that included pictures of Michael when he lived with them. "I thought you and Michael would enjoy these, so I made copies for you. We consider him just as much a son as DJ. So that makes you our daughter-in-law."

"I don't know how to thank you."

"Come see us again. Call if you need anything."

Sera nodded, "I promise." It was a promise she intended to keep.

* * *

It was close to midnight when they all returned to Maui. DJ immediately retired to his room, obviously exhausted. Michael turned to Sera, "How about a late-night motorcycle ride?"

She shook her head no. "Motorcycles scare me. In high school, I had a friend that was killed on a motorcycle. He hit a cow in the middle of the road."

"I don't think we have any cows wandering around Maui, maybe a herd of chickens . . ." Michael smiled at her. "I'm not tired. I'm going out for a while."

Sera was frowning. "Please be careful."

Michael kissed her. "I've done this a thousand times. I'll be fine. Don't worry."

Sera didn't look convinced. "If you're not back in an hour, I'm coming after you."

He laughed. "In an hour, we'll be having some of the best sex of our lives." He kissed her again. "I need something that makes me feel normal. While I can . . ."

Sera nodded. "One hour."

"I'll be back." Then he was gone.

* * *

Joe couldn't sleep. He heard voices and knew everyone was back from Dallas. Anni was fast asleep. He tiptoed downstairs and saw Michael kiss Sera good night. He followed Michael to the garage. "Where are you going, Michael?"

Michael was in a mood he couldn't read. "I'm going out. Wanna come along?"

Joe shook his head no, "I've never been on a motorcycle. Sorry."

"Seriously?" Michael motioned to him. "Let me show you Maui at night."

"I don't know, Michael." There was something about the look that Michael gave him that told him to go, despite all misgivings.

The next thing he knew, they were cruising through the night at warp speed on one of DJ's motorcycles. Michael chose the Hayabusa over the Ducati, since Joe joined him for the ride. To Joe, it was like someone had pushed him out of an airplane, and he was now freefalling to earth. He prayed he had a parachute that actually worked. He flashed back to the kid in the morgue that plowed through a cow. "Slow down, Michael. You're scaring me."

Finally, Michael pulled over. "If you hadn't come with me tonight, I think I would have gone over a cliff. It's not so much that I'm scared of death, but what it's going to take to get to that point."

"Anni is going to have a baby, our baby, Michael."

Michael finally connected with him. "I would never do anything to harm any of you, or myself for that matter."

Joe could finally breathe. "I would hope not. Let's go home. Slower would be nice. Okay?"

He was relieved when Michael nodded in agreement. "I would never entertain that thought, Joe." Michael smiled at him. "I just needed to feel free for a while. Before you knew me, I had a wonderful life. I knew where I was going and had my entire life mapped out. I was content, even happy, and my future was secure. And then cancer came along and changed everything. The world that I had created for myself disappeared, and now I'm making plans to die. Sometimes when I say that out loud, it feels like someone else talking. It's surreal. How do you say good-bye to your whole life?"

"I don't think any of us know that until we are faced with our own fallibility." Joe nodded. "Speaking of that, you scared the hell out of me."

"I'm sorry." Michael laughed. "But admit it, wasn't it just a little bit fun?"

Joe shook his head. "If you think fun equates to fear, Michael."

"I say you did. It's like riding a roller coaster. You're scared, but it's so much fun to have the adventure of that moment. Later, you'll realize it was worth it. C'mon, I'll take you home." This time Michael drove the speed limit.

Chapter 67

Tiptoeing into the darkened bedroom, Joe attempted to slip into bed without waking Anni. Instead, she rolled over and smiled at him, and in a teasing voice said, "Where have you been? It's past your curfew."

He pulled her close. "I'm supposed to tell everyone I was having fun on a motorcycle ride with Michael. But the truth is, I think I saw Jesus waiting on one of those curves."

"You are forbidden to do that again." She took his hand. "Here's why." She placed his hand on her growing tummy. "Feel that, Joe?"

"It's feels like your stomach has the hiccups."

"It's our baby, kicking. He or she has been very active tonight. I've been reading all these baby books, and at first it felt like butterflies, now I can actually feel little kicks."

"I can't wait until next week to see the ultrasound together. Can we actually see the face of our baby?"

Anni kissed him. "Not only that, but they can tell us the sex of the baby. I think I want it to be a surprise. What about you?"

Joe sighed. "I'm not sure. If I found out, and I'd be tempted to blurt it out. I don't know if I could keep that secret."

"Well, it's not like we'll be designing a nursery layout. The baby will just have a corner in our bedroom for now. Though, I have looked at some cribs. Would you like to go shopping tomorrow?"

"Oh, the baby kicked again! That is so amazing, Anni." He still had his hand on her tummy. "Of course, we can go shopping.

I intend to enjoy every moment of this pregnancy with you. But I also can't wait to meet out little son or daughter. Is it too early to think about names?"

"I have some thoughts on that. If it's a girl, I'd like to name her after my mother. Her name was Juliet. But if it's a boy, I think we should name him Michael."

Joe nodded. "Let's definitely not name a girl after my mother. Her name was Ethel."

Anni laughed. "I'd have to agree. No on Ethel."

"But I definitely like Michael. There's no doubt on that one. If it's a boy, it's Michael."

* * *

Over the next months, Joe was mesmerized by the changes in Anni. She was absolutely beautiful, the picture of grace as she carried their baby. He had never loved her more. At night, he curled up next to her and gently massaged her tummy and back. He wanted her to be the picture of relaxed. They took Lamaze classes together so they could experience natural childbirth. She also wanted to breastfeed their baby, so Joe was supportive, even going out and buying her supplies. Thankfully, Michael was doing okay at the moment. But he had Sera now, so, emotionally he was in a good place.

Ironically, Michael was comedy. Tapping her belly like it was a ripe water melon about to burst, he often talked to their baby. "Hey in there, I need some advice. I'm working on a song and need some ideas."

Anni would smack him over the head. "It's a baby, Michael. Not a musician."

"Babies love music." He laughed. "This one has dreadlocks, Anni. He wants to party."

Anni shook her head to indicate no. "Absolutely not. Besides, I think it's a girl."

Michael disagreed. "You're having a boy. He can't wait to terrorize you."

Anni laughed. "You terrify me. My baby is going to be normal."

Michael smiled. "Three years from now, you will think a bomb exploded. Good luck!"

Joe frowned. "What do you mean, Michael?"

"Kids go into this stage where their favorite word is 'no.' Rose is there now. She's driving Gloria insane. I'm just saying, kids are a wild ride. Be prepared."

"Well," Anni said, "our child won't be like that. We will work with him or her."

"Yep," Michael nodded. "That's what we all say. Anyway, good luck with that!" He couldn't stop laughing.

Anni was pissed. "I will work with our baby. It won't be like that."

"Oh yeah." Michael had a bemused look. "Kids are a totally different game. You can't win. They have us wrapped around their fingers. Maybe that's the way it's supposed to be, I don't know. I just know you'd throw yourself under a bus for them. I know that's how I feel about Rose. But she can also drive you to the point of feeling like you'd like to throw yourself under a bus. It's crazy. I never imagined feeling this way, but kids change you, they really do."

Joe stepped in. "I think kids do change you. Thankfully, it happens over time."

Michael agreed. "So true. It evolves. I guess my point is that kids change us, challenge us, and really make us look at ourselves. It's a good thing. I'm sure you will both be good parents."

Chapter 68

One month later

"Michael, wake up." It was Sera.
"What's wrong?"
"We have to go to the hospital."
"Am I sick?"
"No, it's Anni. She's in labor."
"Oh, man." He pulled himself up. "Let's go."

* * *

Anni was admitted to Maui Medical Center. She had a private suite. Outside labor and delivery, Michael, Sera, and DJ were waiting. Anni had definitely decided she didn't want to know the sex of the baby. She wanted to be surprised. It was just a few minutes after midnight, when Joe ushered them into Anni's room.

"It's a boy." He was beaming. "We have a son. Please, let me introduce you to Michael Joseph di Blasio." Anni was cradling the baby in her arms. She smiled at Michael.

"Can I hold him?" Michael sat next to her bed.

Delicately, she placed her son in Michael's arms and was struck by his tenderness. "We named him after you."

"I've had a lot of awards in my life, but this, what an honor." He looked from Anni to Joe. "Thank you." He held the baby for quite a while before handing him back to Anni.

* * *

Once again, Sera and Michael sat patiently before Dr. Bryson. "I wish I had better news."

Michael nodded, swallowing hard. Sera squeezed his hand so hard it hurt. Michael didn't cry because he knew if he did, Sera would shatter and it would fall to him to pick up whatever was left of her.

Dr. Bryson continued, "Despite everything we've tried, the cancer continues to spread into your bones, and there are new lesions on your liver. The CT scan of your brain shows an area of concern and . . ."

"All right. I get the picture." He struggled for composure. "No more. I'm voting for comfortable for as long as possible. How much time do I have?"

"We never know. We're on God's clock, Michael. Maybe six months . . . a year at the most."

"There are no other options for me? Please, Dr. Bryson. I'm only thirty-two years old. I want to live. I have a daughter, Rose."

Dr. Bryson looked close to tears. "I'm so sorry."

"So that's it?" Michael could feel Sera shaking.

"I will order comfort medications and hospice, when that time comes, if you want."

"No more hospitals. I want to stay in my home, with my wife and friends. Privacy is important to me." Turning to Sera, he said. "Let's go home." He looked over at Dr. Bryson. "Thanks for doing everything you could. I just can't keep going through this torture. You do understand?"

She nodded. "I know it's rare, but I'll be checking in on you. I'll stay in touch with Anni, and am willing to make house calls."

Michael nodded. "If you can think of anything else I can do that wouldn't require chemo or radiation . . ."

"I think we've tried everything, Michael. But if I hear of something, I'll let you know."

* * *

When they returned home, Sera went straight up to the lanai to be alone for a while. She felt physically sick from crying so hard. When they had left Dr. Bryson's office, they sat in the car, held each other and cried. Finally, Michael said, "I want to go home."

"Do you want me to drive?"

"Have you ever driven a Lamborghini?"

"No. Why?"

He took a deep quivering breath. "It's okay. It's DJ's car. If I crash it into a tree, he can yell at me."

"Would he really yell at you?"

Michael half-smiled. "Probably after he killed me. That could be Plan B, I guess."

"Please Michael . . ." Sera looked sick.

"I'm sorry. Right now I don't have any rationale thoughts. I'm on autopilot. First, I need to get us home, after that, I can crash for a while and think. I have to figure out what to do next."

* * *

Michael stood quietly watching Joe and Anni in the great room. They were laughing and looked happy together with their baby. Michael thought to himself. *That's how I want to remember them.* Finally, he took a deep breath and walked into the room. "How's my little rock-'n'-roll prodigy?"

"He's such a good baby, Michael." Anni smiled at him. She had just finished nursing the baby and handed him to Joe, who was sitting next to her. "How was your appointment with Dr. Bryson?"

"It could have gone better." Michael was struggling to control his voice.

"What does that mean?" Anni frowned.

Michael reached out and played with baby Michael's chubby fist. "It means that I probably won't see your son's first birthday."

"Oh, Michael," Anni couldn't think. "Oh no, Michael, no."

Joe took him by the arm. "What did the doctor say? What can you do? Surely there is something more you can do?"

"I can't believe this." Michael was choking on his words. "She said something about six months . . . a year if I'm lucky. At this point, I'm not feeling very lucky."

It was like watching the implosion of a building. One minute, it was standing there, the next everything crumpled to the ground in a heap. The only thing left was smoke billowing to the sky. Joe held him as he cried.

Chapter 69

Over the next few months, it seemed difficult to remember that Michael was the same person he'd met a few years ago. Michael was still capable of getting around with minimal assistance, though it was becoming apparent to everyone that he was in more pain. One evening, Michael suggested they all go to dinner. Instead Anni made her famous lasagna. Michael kept shifting and sighing, obviously in distress, barely eating. Finally, he whispered something to Sera. She returned with some pain medicine. Shortly thereafter, he went out by the pool and fell asleep in the hammock.

Joe was sitting beside him when Michael woke. "Hey Joe, what time is it?"

"It's about five in the morning."

"You know, I'm not good at this suffering stoically shit."

"We'll take care of you."

"I don't want to be taken care of, damn it."

"You won't have that choice, Michael."

Michael seemed to be pondering his words. "You know, I've given up a lot since this diagnosis, and I imagine that part isn't going to get better. When I was a child, there were times when I felt vulnerable and powerless. I made a promise to myself that would never happen to me again. But then, life takes you in another direction and along comes the next challenge." Michael smiled slightly. "Sometimes there is incredible power in the grace of letting go. That's what Sera told me."

Joe nodded. "I agree with her, Michael, but it's not always an easy thing to do. Remember when I told you about the accident where my father died?"

"Of course."

"It wasn't the end. It was the beginning. I was with him in heaven. I saw heaven. We walked together, and we talked like we had never done before. The presence of God was always around, and for the first time in my existence, I felt totally at peace. I wanted to stay, but my father told me I had to go back to earth. My mission wasn't done. I cried, Michael. Not because I was losing him, but because I wanted to stay there. My father told me, and now I understand, that others would need me, and now I'm with you and I have a son. I remember my father's hands, pulling me from the wreck, but he couldn't have because he was dead, and yet, I know he was there.

"You said we have angels. Guardian angels and spirit guides. Spirit guides comfort us when we are here, frightened, in pain or in need. I think the guardian angels carry us home. But one day, I have absolutely no doubt, we will be together again. Our spirits are bonded and that is the God, or universal truth in all of us. God gives us the strength to carry each other." He looked over at Michael.

"You never told me that part of the story." Michael smiled. "Those were your guardian angels, Joe. When I get there, I'll send you a sign that all is well. You'll know it when you see it."

Joe traced a tiny cross on Michael's forehead. "A blessing for you."

"You've probably been waiting to do that for a long time, haven't you?"

"May I ask, have you ever been baptized?"

"You just can't help yourself, can you? But I suppose deep inside, you'll always be a priest." Michael chuckled, then sighed. "You'd have to ask Gina. I don't know. Does it matter? Is that another one of those antiquated rules, like you can't get a pass into heaven without it?"

"I'll just ask Gina."

"Well, let's not take any chances. If it's important, just splash some holy water on me, okay?"

Joe shook his head. "I know you don't mean to be sacrilegious. It probably means more to me than it does to you. So to answer your question, yes, it's kind of a rule."

"Well then, go find some holy water. For god's sake, this isn't the time make a catastrophic mistake."

Chapter 70

Dear Great Spirit/God/Whatever you are,

    Let's leave you out of it for a minute and begin with the whole heaven concept. If Joe is right and there is a heaven, I just hope you play good music and know how to have a little fun. Though, I guess I could show you. Is that why you need me so badly? Not that I'm trying to offend you or anything, because I don't want to get kicked over to the dark side, but what's your problem up there? Do you just need a hot guitar player in your celestial band?? Seriously though, I'd like to ask you a couple things. Is this really out of your hands or have we just snowballed everything up so much on earth that you can't fix it? And another thing, do you really pay attention to what we are doing down here? Are you like some drone in the sky, recording everything on a naughty or nice list for later use against us? Is that even fair or logical? Really, I don't think we meant to mess it up down here. Things just got out of control, you know? We probably stopped consulting you. Our bad.

    Anyway, there is one small item I'd like to address in this one-sided conversation. My pain is getting worse by the day. If you could just spare me some anguish, I'd really appreciate it. No more hospitals, okay? Oh yeah, and I'm sure people ask you this all the time, but if it's not too much trouble, can you send down one of my guardian angels with a miracle? I don't expect a cure or even remission, but something tangible would be nice. I'm sure you have a good imagination. After all, you created me, right?

Yours truly, Michael (as in the archangel)

Chapter 71

Two months later

Sera heard Michael whimpering in his sleep. The pain pills were no longer holding down his discomfort. "Michael," she whispered softly. When he didn't respond, she went to find Anni to give him an injection.

Turning on the bedside light, she realized he was awake. "You were crying in your sleep. Anni is here. She can give you something stronger for pain."

"I was trying to get to the bathroom, but I can't move my legs." His voice edged on hysteria. "I can't roll over. It's like I'm numb from the hips down. What's happening now?"

DJ had just returned home and was coming down the hallway when he heard the commotion in Michael's room. "What's wrong?"

Joe arrived. "Anni? What's going on?"

Michael was struggling to get up. "DJ, help me."

Anni adeptly delivered the injection. "You're going to be okay. Probably some pressure on the nerves in your spine. You'll be fine. If it's not better in the morning, we can call Dr. Bryson."

Anni turned to Joe and DJ. "Can you help him into the bathroom?"

DJ nodded. "Why is this bed all wet?"

"Oh my god, now what?" Michael was beyond mortified. "Am I bleeding again?"

Joe attempted to minimize the incident. Turning to Anni, he said, "We need clean sheets."

"Oh, dear god, no . . ." Michael gasped. "This can't be happening to me. Oh god . . . no . . ."

"It's not your fault," Joe tried to offer comfort. "You can't feel anything right now."

Michael put his hands over his face. He choked, "This is worse than death. I have no control over anything in my life. Not anymore. Nothing . . ."

Sera ordered everyone out of the room. "Michael is going to be all right. I'll take care of him."

Joe took DJ by the arm. "Come with me, DJ." He pulled him out of Michael's bedroom. To his surprise, DJ followed him. They sat together in great room. Joe sat silently, as DJ struggled to compose himself. "I don't know what to do anymore, Joe. I'm lost."

Joe wanted to say something encouraging, but was at a loss for words. "I don't know either, DJ. I'm sorry."

"He isn't going to make it, is he?" DJ put his hands over his face. "Don't answer that."

Joe nodded. He was beyond words.

* * *

Dr. Bryson confirmed Anni's suspicions. They devised round-the-clock shifts in order to meet Michael's needs. As for Michael, his world was divided into two categories: agony or drugged delirium.

It was Sera's decision to call Gina.

Joe wanted to score one final point for his friend. He decided to call on Gloria one last time.

* * *

Joe didn't even call until he was outside her gates. Gloria met him at the door. "This is the second time you've shown up at my doorstep. What is it this time?"

"I'm not asking, I'm begging you to let Rose come to Maui. Her father can't travel right now, but he'd love to see her. DJ can fly us back there right now."

"Rose isn't even here. She's with my mother. Actually, I'm leaving tomorrow for New York to get her." She faked a smile. "Tell Michael I'm sorry. Even if I felt magnanimous, which I don't, it's impossible. Besides, why the urgency? Is his cancer worse? Did he send you?"

"No. I came on my own. He doesn't even know I'm here. And yes, he's sick again."

"As a priest, I'd think you could do better than that." She had the ability to speak without ever moving a muscle in her face. "Is this his latest plot to get Rose away from me?"

"Of course not. He would just like to see his daughter."

"Let me think about it." She stepped closer. "Obviously, you would have no idea what it's like to have a child, but I would never just let someone take her away and jet off to Maui with her. What kind of a mother do you think I am? Oh, wait a minute, you listen to Michael and that boorish friend of his, DJ."

"Then you can come with Rose."

"I've never been to Michael's home in Maui." She seemed to be reconsidering. "You said he's sick, so obviously his cancer is back. Define sick."

"Gloria, he's gravely ill."

Gloria softened. "I'm sure he doesn't want to see me. What impact would that have on Rose, seeing her father so sick. I don't know . . ."

"Please, reconsider. Here's my number." He handed her a card. "I won't be back to ask again."

She took his card, turning it over in her hands. Her expression was somber. "Let me think about it."

Joe took a step forward. "You don't have the luxury of time. I'll be blunt. If you wait too long, it could be too late."

Gloria nodded. "What kind of a person would deny him a chance to see his child one more time?"

"Then you will come?"

"I know Michael, and we have had our differences, but I couldn't do this to him or Rose. I know you may not believe this, but I honestly adored him." Gloria's façade crumbled. "We'll be there next week. I don't want to hurt him anymore."

Chapter 72

Sera kissed him on the forehead. "Do you think you can sit in a chair for a little while? Rose will be here in about an hour."

Michael nodded. "I don't want her to see me lying in bed. I want to hold her on my lap. But I'm afraid it's going to be painful. I don't know if I can hide that really well, and I don't want to be stoned on pain medicine."

Anni walked in, "I have an idea. We'll use props. We'll place a pillow on your lap. That way she won't be sitting directly on you. Then, we can drape a blanket over you. I'll give you something for pain, but I'll just give you a half dose."

"I guess that could work. At least it's a plan." He noticed his hands were shaky. "I'll give you a sign if it's just too much."

"One more thing," Sera said, "what about Gloria?"

"Let's not give her a show. She can stay in the great room."

* * *

Anni escorted Gloria and Rose into the house. "You can stay here, Gloria." She pointed to the great room. "Would you like something to drink?"

"No, thank you." She quietly sat down on one of the sofas, looking around her surroundings. "It's beautiful." Then she turned to Rose. "Your daddy is sick. Be a good girl." She gave her daughter a hug. Then, she nodded to Anni. "If it's too much on her, bring her back."

"I'll stay with her." Anni took her little hand. "Let's go visit with your daddy."

* * *

"Daddy!" She ran across the room, her arms outstretched, then suddenly stopped.

"It's okay, dolly. It's me. I've just been sick." Michael put out his arms for her. Anni helped the little girl onto his lap. Sera sat quietly across the room, watching the reunion of father and daughter. Rose looked very much like her mother, with blonde hair and blue eyes. But she had her father's broad smile. He smiled back at her.

"Hey, Rose," Michael hugged her to him. "Look at you." She was wearing an orange tutu, a floppy Easter hat, and pink sandals. "Love the outfit. I'll bet you picked it out yourself, huh?"

"Pretty for you, Daddy. I have sunglasses, too." She was carrying a little purse and pulled out a little pair of pink sunglasses. She put them on to show him, only they were upside down. She smiled proudly. She hopped down and started to dance.

"That's definitely my girl." Michael laughed. "I'm guessing pink is your favorite color?"

"Purple and pink." She started to bounce. "I like books. Can you read me a story?"

Michael turned to Sera. "We have that covered, right?"

Sera smiled. "We do. Your daddy has presents for you."

She was headed straight for Sera. Michael took a deep breath.

Anni asked quietly, "Doing okay?"

Michael nodded. "Okay."

Unwrapping her presents, she stopped when she got to books. She ran back to Michael. "This one. Please." She crawled back onto his lap. For the next half hour, he read one book after another to her. Rather than having her getting on and off of his lap, Sera sat next to them, handing the books to them, one at a time.

In the meantime, Gloria decided to explore. She stopped before the shelves of pictures and awards. There were even a few pictures with her and Michael, back in the days when they were still together. Of course, there were pictures of Rose scattered throughout. Glancing at her watch, she saw that Rose had been with Michael for over an hour. It must be going well.

The pool area looked inviting, so she wandered out there. She looked around for security cameras and adeptly stayed away from their watchful eyes. There was a small path that led away from the pool, so she followed it through a lush garden and fountains. Beyond that point, there was another patio with ceiling fans and a perfect view of the ocean. She walked over to the patio and heard Rose laughing, she stopped.

Carefully making her way closer, she realized the patio was an extension of Michael's bedroom. The sliding glass walls were open and a soft breeze was blowing a light curtain. She inched closer, staying a safe distance away, but hidden from their view. She saw Michael sitting in a chair, a blanket draped over his lap. She caught her breath.

He looked emaciated and washed out to the point of being translucent. The only color was from his green silk robe. She watched him turning the pages in a book he was reading to Rose. His hands were skeletal and shaking. Every now and then, she could hear his voice. He sounded weary, and a little slurred, which she assumed was due to medication.

Rose hopped off his lap, and Michael shifted as if he was trying to get comfortable. Anni came over and adjusted a pillow behind his back. Sera took over reading the rest of the book to Rose. She didn't know this Michael, and if she could have, she would have gone over and given him a hug. Wiping away tears, she turned and walked away. She wanted to remember the man laughing and dancing in the pictures on the shelves, not the frail person that could barely sit in his chair. She whispered to herself, "I'm sorry, Michael. If only I could turn back time."

Michael finally gave Anni a nod. "One more hug, dolly."

She gave him a big hug and kiss. "Bye-bye, Daddy. See you latergater."

"Bye-bye, dolly." Michael was fighting back tears. He knew it was probably the last time he ever saw his little daughter. "I love you." It was all he could think to say to her.

When Anni entered the great room, Gloria was standing, staring out the window at the ocean. She looked like she had been crying. "Could I have just one minute with him? There's something I'd like to tell him."

Anni hesitated. "He's very tired and not feeling well. I don't know . . ."

Gloria choked back a sob. "I came all this way. Please. I just want to tell him I'm sorry."

Anni shook her head. "I'll go ask him. Stay here." She went back to his room. He was half-asleep in the chair. "Gloria wants to tell you she's sorry."

"Okay." He closed his eyes.

"No, I mean she wants to tell you in person."

Michael let out a ragged sigh. "I'm not in any mood for her drama. Tell her I accept her apology, and I'm sorry, too. Maybe next time . . . oh, and thank her for bringing Rose. That little miracle meant a lot to me."

Anni went back down the hall and gave Gloria the message.

"All right. I understand." Gloria took Rose's hand. "Come on, honey. Let's go home."

Chapter 73

When Gina arrived, she was not prepared for what was before her. She turned to Anni. "What has happened here?" It sounded more like an accusation than a question. She hugged Michael, and he cried out in pain.

"I should have warned you." Anni tried to explain. "Even the slightest touch causes him pain. His bones are very brittle."

"You mean I could have cracked his bones?" Gina was almost hysterical. "I can't imagine he's so sick that he can't even turn over in his own bed!"

Anni pointed to the IVs. "Michael is heavily sedated and feels minimal pain."

"But why did he cry out like that? Did I hurt him?"

"We can't relieve him of all his pain, Gina. The best we can do is to make him comfortable."

Gina burst into tears. "He needs to be in a hospital."

"He refuses to go to the hospital again. He wants to stay at home."

"Oh my god." Gina lowered herself into the nearest chair. "Show me what to do."

* * *

Joe offered to take a turn on the night shift with Michael. Besides, Anni needed a break, as the baby had been fussy with an ear infection, and she needed to care for baby Michael. DJ had to leave for a few days, and Sera hadn't slept in almost twenty-four hours. Gina was dozing in a chair, next to Michael's bed.

He was surprised to see Michael was awake, watching him.

"Hey, Michael." Joe stroked his forehead.

"I need you to do something for me."

"Of course."

"I don't want to bother Sera, but could you please handle the arrangements? I've taken care of everything with my attorneys. There are copies of all the necessary documents in the desk in my studio." Michael was breathing as if he couldn't get enough air. "Just make it something simple and private. No big funeral. Funerals are so morbid and depressing. No one needs that shit. Don't let it turn into a side show. Sera can't handle that." He looked over at his sister. "And neither can Gina. Look at her. She almost looks as bad as me."

"Whatever you want, Michael."

He nodded. "Okay. And another thing . . ."

Joe nodded.

Michael seemed close to blacking out. "This is gonna be rough on Sera . . . take care of her for me."

"I promise you, Michael." Tears streamed down his face. "Anything else?"

"Remove the mirrors. I can't stand to look at my reflection anymore."

* * *

"When you turn him on his side, place a pillow between his knees; that takes pressure off, so we don't have to worry about sores, then I snuggle a pillow against his back for support."

Michael listened to Anni's voice in a vacuum. He wanted all of them to go away, but couldn't think of the words. He tried to push them away with his hand. He didn't want anyone touching him. It hurt too much.

"Michael, Gina's here." Anni saw the expression on his face. "Pain makes him intolerant, Gina. Sometimes he won't even let DJ touch him. He said he hurts him."

"I can't do this." Gina burst into tears. "Oh Michael . . . baby . . . I can't watch this . . ." She ran from the room.

Michael finally recognized the voice as Gina's. "It's okay. If I could, I'd go with you."

Sera tiptoed in and helped Anni position him on his side. Sera added, "I'll finish his bath." She knew the medication was wearing off, and it wasn't time for his next dose. Michael always cried out in pain when they turned him. It was probably better that Gina wasn't there for that.

Sera was physically and emotionally wiped out. After getting him settled, she crashed into a bed. Joe was taking care of the baby so Anni could handle Michael's needs at night, which was now a fulltime job. DJ returned and never left, making it clear he would stay to the end. He called his father to let him know he wouldn't be back for a while. Business would have to wait.

* * *

Joe had put baby Michael to bed and wanted some peace. Instead, he heard a woman weeping inconsolably on the lanai. Instinctively, he knew it was Gina. He put his arm around her. "I'm sorry, Gina."

"I had the right to know he was so sick. Maybe I could have done something."

"Michael didn't want to burden you."

"I guess I should be grateful Sera called me. Michael should know that he would never be a burden to me."

"Have you ever told him the truth, Gina?" Joe pressed. "I think he has the right to know."

"No, I've always been so embarrassed. Back then, I was a mess. I'd made so many mistakes. I actually thought it would be better for him to believe my mother was the parent. And now, here we are today. My child, my son, is dying." She was sobbing. "I feel so guilty because I was an awful mother to him. I'm so sorry . . ."

"Guilt is killing you, Gina. You did the best you could." Joe said. "Trust me. You let DJ's family help him. He wouldn't have all this today, if it weren't for your sacrifices for him."

"How did you know that?"

"I know Michael's story. He loves you. You love him. I'm surprised you don't realize that. But if you can't tell him you are his mother and that you're sorry he had a rough childhood, then you need to find a way to let go of your guilt. It's up to you now."

"He's not really dying, is he, Father Joe?" Her face crumbled. "Not my Michael."

"I think you'll be able to tell him the truth. I believe in you."

"I will." She nodded. "I promise this time I'll do it right."

Chapter 74

"Oh Joe, can you help me turn Michael onto his side?" Anni looked exhausted.

"Which way are we going?"

"To the right."

"Where's Sera?"

"She's been sick all day."

"Is she ill or is it stress?"

Anni gave him a side glance. "What do you think?"

Joe nodded. "Where's DJ and Gina?"

"I haven't had time to hunt them down."

Michael was awake and aware. "DJ and Gina can't handle this. I say we give them some something else to do."

Joe tenderly touched Michael's arm. "How are you doing today, my friend?"

"I've been better, Joe." He attempted a faint smile. "Sorry about Gina. I told you she wasn't good at this stuff. It's why I always gave her a pass."

"I know. She needs to talk to you."

"What about?"

"She has something she needs to tell you."

"Just give me the cliff notes. I'm beyond a Springer moment."

"She can tell you. It's not my place."

"If it's that she is actually my mother, I figured that out years ago." Michael sighed. "She needs to stop feeling guilty. People make mistakes. I don't care and never did. I'm just glad someone cared enough to love me. She did her best, and for that, I love her. Her job is done."

Joe stepped back. "But, Michael, you need to let her tell you. It's important to her."

Michael nodded. "Okay. Bring her in."

Gina had quietly stepped into the room and heard his last comment. "But how did you know?"

"All I had to do was look at your face every time you looked at me. That's all I needed to know." Michael reached for her hand.

"I'm so sorry for everything. I acted out of love, Michael."

"It's okay, Gina. I'm not angry with you."

"You have every right to hate me. I did it all wrong, and I'm so sorry."

"Please don't do this to yourself."

"But I can't bear the guilt anymore." She was sobbing uncontrollably. Tenderly gathering him in her arms, she rocked him gently. Her baby. "I never meant to hurt you, and now, I feel like I'm somehow responsible for all of this. Please tell me I'm forgiven."

"No need to apologize, Gina."

"Tell me what to do."

"Just stay with me. That's all I want from you now."

"Oh, Michael, my baby . . . I love you more than you'll ever know."

"I do know. It's okay." Michael looked close to passing out on her.

Anni injected some medication into his IV. He relaxed and let the drug go to work, sinking deeper, his mind went blank. He felt nothing until it was time to be turned again. This time, it was DJ and Gina. He cried out as they awkwardly turned him onto his left side and accidentally dropped him. He was jolted back to reality and cried out in pain.

* * *

"Is something wrong?" Joe was shocked to see Dr. Bryson when he arrived home from mass.

Dr. Bryson didn't like the daily updates from Anni. So she decided to arrange a visit. "Luckily, there doesn't appear to be any broken bones, but this self-styled treatment must stop. We can arrange for hospice to come and help. Can't you see he needs more care? He isn't thinking clearly. So you must decide for him. I don't think you want to be responsible for this."

"It's up to Michael." Sera was adamant. "He doesn't want to go to the hospital again."

Dr. Bryson shook her head. "We can set up hospice in the home."

"We can handle it." It was Sera that spoke up. "He wants his privacy. So we'll figure it out."

Dr. Bryson nodded. "I don't agree, but I guess I have to defer to the patient and family. Call if you need me." With that, she left.

Chapter 75

The pain was holding steady. He now had a pump that automatically dispensed medication, so there was no need for injections. Even with the pump in place, it barely took the edge off his pain. "I can't do this much longer, Sera."

"Hush, Michael. Don't talk like that."

"I know I'm dying." It sounded like an actor in a movie just uttered those words.

"You've just suffered a setback, that's all."

"I've suffered enough and it's more than a setback, Sera. Death will be a blessing."

"Oh no, Michael . . . please . . . hold on . . ."

"What day is it? It must be close to Christmas."

"It's December 15." Sera sat next to him.

"Is the sun shining?"

"No, it's raining, honey."

Michael nodded. "Will you lay down with me? It's been such a long time . . ."

Sera carefully slipped onto the bed, trying to avoid the IVs and not to hurt him.

"Did we ever make the popcorn and fudge?"

"No, but it's okay. I love you, Michael." Gently, she held him in her arms. "I understand you're ready to give up, but I can't." She choked back sobs. "When I lose you, my heart will go with you. I'll never love anyone again."

"Don't do that, Sera. I know that scared little girl inside, and it's not worth being sick. My wish for you is to be happy again, to have children, to live life to your fullest potential. That would make me happy."

"But I can't do that without you." She was sobbing.

"You can't see it now, but I promise, someday you will love again, and when you do, I'll know it doesn't mean you love me any less. It will mean that together, we learned how to love. I will always watch over you. Whenever you think of me, I'll be there, Sera."

Chapter 76

"**Forgive me, Michael**." Nervously, Joe sat the tiny vial of holy water on the bedside table. It was past midnight and his turn to stay with Michael for the night. Sera was fast asleep in a rocking chair across the room. Carefully, he opened the bottle and dipped his fingers in the holy water. The clock on the wall kept time with the drip of the intravenous line. Joe made the sign of the cross and gently laid his hands on Michael's head. "I baptize you in the name of the Father, and the Son, and Holy Ghost. Amen." Under the circumstances, that was good enough. Joe took a deep breath. Michael continued to sleep.

Chapter 77

Anni had never participated in a less joyous Christmas Eve. They all gathered at Michael's bedside in a candlelight vigil. Michael had taken a turn for the worse, and Dr. Bryson offered no hope of Michael living more than a few days. His breathing was labored and erratic. Anni monitored his blood pressure, which continued to freefall.

Michael opened his eyes and looked at each of them. "Stay with me. I don't want to be alone. Not tonight."

Joe blinked back tears. "I won't leave you, Michael."

DJ bolted from the room. "I can't handle this." A door slammed and a motorcycle rumbled to life.

Michael's eyes followed him out the door.

Sera and Gina were on either side of his bed, holding his hands. They were both quietly crying.

Joe prayed in silence. *Dear Lord, Grant him peace . . .*

Michael whispered. "It doesn't hurt as much anymore. I just feel like going to sleep."

"Then go to sleep, Michael." Joe struggled not to cry.

Michael looked to her. "Seraphine?"

"I'm here, Michael."

Michael closed his eyes. "Tell me a story, Sera. I want to hear your voice."

Sera laid her head on his chest. It comforted her to feel his breath in her hair and hear his heart flutter against her ear. She whispered softly to him.

"There was once a woman who was carrying twin babies. The first baby was an optimist, but his twin was more pessimistic. The one named Optimistic told his brother, very soon we will be going on a journey together, and I'm so excited because even though we will be going through some hard times, it's going to be worth it, because on the other side, there is a whole new world waiting for us.

"Pessimistic replied to his brother, what I've heard is that we are going to go through something called birth, and that it will be painful and frightening. Once we come into this new world, we are greeted by loud noise, bright lights and unlike the womb, it is cold there.

"But Optimistic smiled at his brother. No dear brother, the truth is that the pain is all worth it. The loud noises are laughter and tears from those who have been joyously waiting to welcome us. The light is the sun rising and the moon in the night. The arms that are waiting to hold us are warm and strong, so that when we feel weak or small, they can carry us home . . ."

Michael's hand still clung limply to Gina. Anni sat at the foot of his bed, gently rocking her baby in her arms. Joe watched his breathing become slower and more shallow. Sera stirred from a light sleep. Something told her there had been a shift in her world. Then she realized she could no longer feel his breath or hear his heart beating into her ear.

It was finished. His suffering was over.

Whimpering softly, Sera clung to him until the early light of dawn.

Candles burned out and left puddles of warm wax. Anni gave Sera a sedative and took her down the hall to sleep. It was Christmas morning, and while the rest of the world celebrated, Joe was busy handling the necessary details. There would be no celebration in this house today.

Chapter 78

The house was still, curtains drawn. DJ was surprised to hear the doorbell ring. Would the press be so callous to push in on them today? Surely, they could leave them alone for one day. He didn't feel up to answering their stupid questions. Closing his eyes, he chose to ignore the door. Whoever it was could wait until he was ready. Maybe in a year or two . . .

The doorbell rang again. Whoever it was remained persistent. Finally, Joe went to answer the door. He didn't want them to disturb Sera. Opening the door, he was greeted by Gloria and Rose. He was too wasted to register emotion.

"We wanted to surprise Michael." Gloria was obviously proud to be so generous. "Rose and Michael need to spend some time together. Christmas seems like a good time for daddy-and-daughter time again."

Sera heard voices and stumbled to the door. Still under the influence of the sedatives, she had no idea how ravaged she looked. Nothing mattered anymore. She stared blankly at Gloria. "You're too late, Gloria." Her voice was flat. "I'm sorry. Michael died last night."

Gloria looked stunned. "Michael's gone?"

Rose reached out, laughing. "Daddy! I'm here, Daddy! I'm back."

Sera turned away so Rose couldn't see her face.

Joe tried for composure, but lost it. "I'm so sorry, Rose." She wouldn't understand that her daddy wasn't coming back.

"Oh no . . ." Gloria's tough demeanor crumbled. "Oh no . . . not Michael . . ."

Joe managed to nod. "Yeah." He couldn't grasp it yet. He took her by the arm. "Come in, Gloria." He closed the door behind her.

* * *

Later that day, Joe went down the hall and paused outside Michael's door. Taking a deep breath, he forced himself to go inside. He tried to avoid staring at the empty bed. A mound of blankets were pushed aside, as if someone had simply left in a great hurry without taking time to make the bed. Wrapping his arms around the comforting pile of blankets, he wept shamelessly until he cried himself to sleep.

Chapter 79

One month later

Tiny golden aspen leaves shimmered brightly against the backdrop of majestic mountains and blueberry Colorado skies. The air was so cool and crisp that it hurt to breathe. A light dusting of snow powdered the ground during the night. Sera strolled in silence along the path leading back to the log home. She didn't see the beauty of the mountains or the brilliant colors. It had been almost a month since Michael's death, and she still felt lost and disorganized.

Fortunately, no one paid any attention to her. She was just the eccentric widow of *the* Michael Dolanski. And that was now yesterday's news. There were many long, cold nights where she cried herself to sleep, clutching his green silk robe, because it still had the scent of his cologne. She had packed all of Michael's clothes and hung them in the closet as if he would be home any day. Only that never happened. Michael wasn't coming back this time.

The home in Maui was sold last week. DJ considered keeping it, then changed his mind. Too many sad memories, I guess. For now, he moved back home to Texas. The band was still trying to regroup, but DJ had decided that he didn't want to be part of it anymore. The fun was gone.

Gina returned home. Rumor had it that she was engaged. Sera hoped she was finally happy and had found someone to love. Everyone deserves to be loved by someone.

Sauntering into the living room, she curled up in Michael's blankets and once again watched the videos of Michael playing in the band. She smiled, and Michael smiled back at her. She enjoyed seeing him, vibrant again, singing and laughing. Then, he spun away. Gone again. Someone else in the band took his place. No. Please, come back. She turned it off.

On the table, she picked up her cell phone and sent the text she had been writing to Joe and Anni:

In your last message, you sounded concerned about me. Don't be. I'm fine. The mountains are beautiful. Peaceful. A lovely retreat from the world . . .

Then she cried. Again.

* * *

Before the house in Maui sold, they all gathered: Sera, DJ, Gina, Joe, and Anni all strolled down to the beach for the last time. It was sunset. The colors in the sky looked like a mosaic painted by a poet's hand. Each took a handful of ashes and tossed them into the ocean. The wind carried them away. They sat there until a sliver of the moon showed its pale face and stars freckled the night sky in brilliant abundance. Baby Michael peacefully slept in his mother's arms.

Sera finally spoke. "I'm going for a walk. I need to be alone."

Joe nodded. "Me too."

They both went in separate directions.

Epilogue

Joe knelt in prayer in the sand. "Hey, Michael, I know you can hear me, but I just wanted to let you know that Anni and I are okay down here. It's not the same though. Sometimes I can feel your presence as if you're standing next to me. But you promised to give me a sign. More than ever, I need that tonight." Joe fought back tears.

"God, I miss you. This is the only way I can talk to you now." He could taste his tears. He put his hands over his face, now sobbing. "You were my best friend, Michael. I was supposed to help you, but all along, you were helping me. Please, Michael. You promised me. Give me something."

He looked to the sky and saw a falling star. Then another one, and then another, like a private meteor shower, just for his viewing. "Thank you, Michael. Thank you." For a long time, he sat alone on the beach, mesmerized by the moment, like a child watching fireworks for the first time.

The following day, the news reported it was an unusual phenomenon, unexpected and unexplainable, and that scientists believed it was a meteor that had shattered into several pieces as it passed through the night. But Joe understood and knew it wasn't a random coincidence. He didn't believe in those anymore.

* * *

Sera walked to a quiet place, away from everyone. It was a place where she and Michael had come many times, meditated, and made love together. Raising her arms to the sky, she lifted her face to heaven. She stood beneath the starlit night as the meteor shower lit up the night, tears streaming down her face. "We will always be connected, Michael. I hear your voice in the waves and in the wind. I feel your presence with me every day." It was a private moment, between her and Michael, as she released the rest of his ashes to the wind. "I release you to the universe. But I will love you with every breath I take, until the day I die and beyond the stars in the sky. You will live forever in my heart."